DRIFTER
PART TWO

DRIFTER

PART TWO

DAVID
ARCHER

"...THE NEXT JACK REACHER!"

1

There are men in our world who are darker and more evil than most people will ever imagine. Even those who have come across them have a tendency towards disbelief, allowing themselves to deny even the evidence of their own senses.

Sam Prichard didn't have that luxury. He was a man who had to face reality, even when reality was something he'd rather ignore.

"Okay," Ken said, "so what you need to understand is who the kings of the north and south are. The king of the North is Russia. The king of the South, on the other hand, is old Babylon, which we now call Iraq. They will form an alliance and will move to make war against the nation of Israel. According to the Bible, that will be the final battle before Christ comes again."

Sam shook his head. "So, what you're telling me is that all these nations that have been following the

1

Antichrist, the Beast, will turn against him? But I thought he was supposed to be the great ruler, the one who would come and fix all the problems of the world?"

Nodding his head, Ken said, "Right, that's how the world will see him, at first. He'll be the one to bring peace to the Middle East, by creating a peace treaty with Israel that will seem to solve all the problems that have plagued the region all these years. The problem comes in when he decides that he's more than just a leader, and actually demands that people worship him as if he were God. That's when the ten kings, the ten nations that had been backing him until that point, will rebel against him. He will have established his headquarters in Jerusalem by that point, so in order to attack him, his enemies will invade Israel."

"And Israel is special to God, so He won't allow it to be destroyed, right?"

Ken nodded again. "Exactly," he said. "According to Bible prophecy, that will be one of the bloodiest battles ever fought on earth. The blood of the soldiers who die will run in streams, it says, as deep as a horse's bridle, but Israel will not be defeated."

Sam looked up at him. "And at this point, Christ returns to rule the earth?"

"Yep," Ken said. "That's how it works out. Now, I don't know if we're actually coming up to that point or not, but I do know that an awful lot of the things that have to happen to allow this to occur have happened.

There are only a few things left, according to prophecy, that have not yet taken place. One of those, of course, is the rise of the Beast, the Antichrist himself. Our guy Chandler, who apparently follows a different view of how these prophecies all play out, is trying to maneuver himself into a position that will allow him to control that Beast when he appears. In biblical prophecy, this would seem to mean that Chandler is the person referred to as the false prophet. The false prophet, and I don't claim to understand how all this works, is the one who will be telling people what to do in the name of the Beast, wielding both political and religious power. It looks like Chandler wants that job."

"And in order to get it," Sam said, "he needs to bring on the one world government, the New World order or whatever it's called, so that he can figure out whose strings it is he's planning to pull. Right?"

"Bingo!" Ken said, pointing a finger at Sam. "But I don't think he's just waiting to find out who it is, I think he's trying to put someone in that position."

"Wouldn't that be going against the prophecies? Trying to overrule God?"

"Not necessarily," Ken said. "If Chandler is the false prophet, if he is the one who was destined by these prophecies to fulfill that position, then it's quite likely that he's doing exactly what God would want him to do. I mean, that would be his place in all of this. My position is simply that, if he's just a wannabe, as I think he is, then he needs to be stopped. Frankly, I've read these prophecies over and over, and there are still things that need to happen before we reach that time. In my opinion, Chandler is trying to bypass those things and make it happen sooner. If that's the case, then I don't think God will mind if we put a stop to Chandler's plans."

Sam leaned back against the wall. He was sitting on the bed in the motel room they had gotten the night before, in order to get some rest before they made it into DC. No matter how things went when they got there, they knew it wasn't going to be pleasant. Chandler wanted them dead, and there was very little doubt that he had a number of assassins out on the prowl, looking for them.

"Taking down a guy like Chandler isn't going to be easy," Sam said. "We're talking about an experienced CIA agent, and from what Harry says, he's a pretty dangerous man himself. Even without his goons, there's a good chance that he could spot us coming and take us out before we can get to him. Is that right?"

Ken smiled grimly. "He's a badass, all right. I doubt there are any official records of how many people he's killed, but I'd personally bet that it would go over a hundred. As for those whose deaths he has ordered, I'd probably put that number well over a thousand. In his position, Chandler can order the elimination of minor functionaries in just about any country that his desk oversees. Now, it's a common practice to cultivate those functionaries by letting them see how easy it is to have them killed. What you do is, you approach one of their assistants and ask him or her if they would like to have their boss's job. You may have to go through a few of them before you find the one who says yes, but then you simply eliminate the boss and everyone under the boss who is over the one you made the deal with. Now you've got someone in that position you, A, owes you a huge favor; B, knows you can have him or her killed as easily as you got rid of those above them; and C, is therefore not even inclined to risk pissing you off. Chandler probably has dozens, if not hundreds of those people in place in different countries, so it's highly likely that he can arrange just about anything he wants, and just about anywhere in the world."

Sam shook his head. "No man should have that much power," he said. "No wonder this guy has a God complex. He feels like he can do anything already, and get away with it."

"And the worst part of that? He's right," Ken said. "I would just about bet you that Harry is the first person Chandler's gone after who wasn't dead an hour later. This guy is accustomed to getting what he wants, and what he wants right now is all of us out of his hair. The sooner we can either expose him or kill him, the more likely it becomes that you and I will live to see another sunrise."

Sam sat forward, turned and put his feet on the floor. "Just because I'm the curious sort, what kind of odds would you give us as it stands right now?"

Ken shrugged. "Right now? Maybe one chance in thirty. As much as I hate to say it, it's not very likely that we're going to find anyone on Capitol Hill who doesn't owe him some pretty big favors. Now, what that means is that anyone we approach is probably going to be afraid to have anything to do with us. By that, I mean that they will be a lot more afraid of making Chandler mad at them than they would be of not doing the right thing by helping us expose him. Right and wrong are not the same concepts on Capitol Hill that they are in the rest of the world; while we might see getting rid of Chandler as the right thing to do and a good thing for our country, most of our senators and congressmen would see it as losing the guy who can fix any problem they run into. To them, that would be about as wrong as it could get. Politics needs people like Chandler, and politicians need him even more."

"So what you're telling me," Sam said, "is that if I go to my Congressman tomorrow and say that I've got evidence that Chandler is committing treason against our country, he's more likely to pick up the phone and tell Chandler I'm there than he is to help me put a stop to Chandler's plans. Is that how it works?"

"Yeah, that's pretty much it."

Sam put his elbows on his knees and rested his face in his hands. The thought crossed his mind that he had never been so angry and so scared at the same time.

"Then we have to kill him." It wasn't a question; it was a statement.

Ken nodded again. "Yes. We have to kill him. I'm sorry, Sam, I know this isn't the world you're used to, but it's the one you blundered into. If I thought I could actually do this alone, I'd drop you off somewhere to hide out until it's over, but Chandler is probably the most dangerous target I've ever taken aim at. I need help, and I need backup. And, if the worst-case scenario happens and I end up dead, I need you to get to Chandler and finish the job."

Sam looked up at him. Only a couple of days ago, Ken Long was nothing but a man whose daughter wanted to talk to him, and so she hired Sam to find him. That's what private eyes do, so Sam took the job. Little did he know that he was buying himself a ticket into the *Twilight Zone*, where men tried to manipulate not only other men, but even the gods into doing their will. Now Sam, who considered himself to be only moderately religious, had been drawn into a plot that was straight out the book of Revelation in the Bible.

* * * * *

Grayson Chandler worked for the CIA, running the Senior Islamic Analysis Desk. What that meant was that he controlled a fairly large room where top analysts said and did nothing but go over intelligence regarding Islamic activities, and particularly those involved with terrorism and anti-Semitic or anti-Christian activities. It was his job to take the information his underlings brought to him and decide what parts of it should be sent on to other agencies, or up to the President of the United States. His reports always got top priority, because if anyone was going to spot an impending terror attack, it was likely to be him or one of his people.

This position made it possible for him to gain lots of leverage in countries that were likely to be targets of Islamic terrorism, as well as countries where Islam, whether extreme or fundamental, was the prevalent religion. In the former, leaders courted his friendship in order to be warned of upcoming activities that could affect their nations; in the latter, they did so in order to be made aware of military or clandestine activities designed to limit or eliminate Islamic power. Either way, Chandler was the man that everybody wanted on their side.

This made him an extremely powerful man, but it wasn't enough for him. Like everyone who has tasted great power, he desired even more and planned all of his activities accordingly. In nearly forty years of service, the last thirty of which had been with the CIA, he had developed an incredible instinct for choosing future power players. It was said that if Chandler favored you, then you were destined for great things. The only question was what his favor was going to cost, because it always came with a price.

Somewhere in those years, Chandler had become aware of the Prophecies Desk, another section that was devoted to the study and analysis of religious prophecy. He had managed to get himself transferred into that section for a few years, back in the early nineties, and he used the time wisely. That section was run by an eight-man panel headed by Professor Isaac Lambert, one of the world's leading experts on the subject. He had spent many hours with Lambert, making certain that he understood all of the different viewpoints related to prophecy and how it affected the United States of America. This included Judaic, Islamic and Christian prophecies, as well as those from some even more obscure religions. Some of the most intriguing prophecies came from the ancient Babylonian and Mesopotamian religions, and those were the ones that Chandler found most interesting.

Of particular interest were some of the unusual prophecies relating to the Babylonian sun god, Shamash. While some Mesopotamian scholars considered him a minor deity, there were many experts in the field who believed that Shamash should be regarded as the supreme being. Because there were so many deep references that made such an implication, there were even those who believed that Shamash should be considered the foundation upon which the Hebrew God, Jehovah, was created.

By following their reasoning, as well as spending time studying with some of Shamash's followers, Chandler had come to the conclusion that Shamash was the Great God who would eventually rule the world. Because certain prophecies relating to him seemed to follow the general outline of the biblical prophecies — although with Shamash being placed as the power behind the one that Bible prophecy referred to as the Antichrist and an entirely different outcome that left that powerful figure in control of the civilized world — Chandler had decided that he had the opportunity to seize control and install himself high in the councils of Shamash.

Of course, he fully understood the way the rest of the world would see him, and he didn't care. What did it matter to him how he might be perceived by those whom he would one day rule? At this point, all he cared about was establishing his power. Yes, that meant following along with Christian prophecy to a point, but that was simply because the future, as he saw it, would progress along a similar path. The journey didn't concern him; all he cared about was the final destination, and that's where he intended to be victorious.

It was incredible, he thought, knowing the future and how it would turn out. It made him wonder just how stupid his enemies could become, to try to keep him from achieving that which had been predestined for thousands of years. Sometimes it actually made him laugh, and he understood completely what Shakespeare's Puck meant when he stated, "Lord, what fools these mortals be!"

* * * * *

"Okay, so we have to kill him, there's no way around

it, right?" Sam asked. "You know, it's a little hard for me to get my mind wrapped around the idea that I'm on the way to commit a murder. I mean, I've always been the guy who tried to prevent such things, y'know? How am I supposed to justify to myself the idea that I have to go and take a man's life in order to do what's right? Can you explain that to me? Because I'm not having any luck trying to figure it out on my own!"

"Youngster, you just hit on the dilemma that faces every assassin on his first mission. No matter how much training he's had, no matter how many times it's been explained to him why he has to do the job he does, he still has to figure out how to justify it to himself. It's one of the most difficult things any man can do, and he has to do it on his own, no one can do it for him."

Sam looked at Ken, and shook his head. "You're not helping. I'm trying to cope with this, and you're not helping."

Ken shrugged, and chuckled at Sam. "What did I just tell you?" he asked. "This is not something anyone can do for you, or even help you to accomplish, you've got to figure it out on your own. The question is simple enough: Which is more important? This man's life or saving your country? Once you figure that out, you'll know the answer. Then you can decide where you stand on the question."

Sam started to answer, but that's when his phone rang, and he lifted it to see that it was Indie calling. He held up a finger to tell Ken to be quiet, then answered. "Well, hello, Gorgeous," he said.

"Hey, Baby," Indie said. "Just wondered how you're doing this morning, and thought I'd give you a call. I miss you, and Kenzie says to tell you she loves you."

"Babe, I miss you and Kenzie more than you can possibly imagine," Sam said. "The more I learn about this mess, the more I wish I'd never returned Joellyn's phone call. I mean, I just don't see me as the guy who's supposed to figure out how to stop the Antichrist, but somehow I got stuck with the job. Do me a favor and call Caleb and see if he has any advice on how to deal with the Antichrist and the false prophet."

Indie laughed, but there wasn't a lot of humor in it. "I'll call him if you want, but are you sure you want anybody to know what you're into right at the moment? From what you've said, this almost sounds like one of those things Harry refers to as so classified you have to be dead to read it."

"Yeah, good point," Sam said. "No sense getting Caleb involved in this insanity with me. So how's everything going there? You staying safe?"

"Ha! Harry added extra security, after he found out who you're dealing with. There's a small army camped outside the cabin right now. Mom and Grace are having fun, running outside and passing out coffee and cookies. I don't think either of them has ever had so much male attention, and they're just not sure how to handle it."

"Yeah, well, as long as those guys know not to mess with you, you're okay. If any of them starts flirting, just remind them that Harry owes me favors. That should be enough to scare them half to death, so they'll back off quick. And if that doesn't work, just sic Beauregard on them. Nobody can stand up to him."

"Sam," Indie said, "tell me you're going to come back to me. Tell me you're going to come back safe."

"Of course I am, Babe," Sam replied. "Nothing else Harry's thrown at me has been able to kill me, so I'm pretty sure this one won't do it, either. I'll be home, and tell Kenzie that I'll do my best not to get shot again. I know how she worries when I get shot."

"Well, gee, I wonder why that would worry her," Indie said. "I mean, it's not like I ever worry about things like that, now do I? No, not me, not ever!"

Sam smiled into the phone. "Baby," he said, "I promise you I'll be away, and home safe. One way or another, as soon as this is over, I'm coming home to you. All the Antichrists and terrorists in the world can't keep me away. I love you, Baby."

"I love you, too, Sam. You came along and turned my whole world upside down, and now I don't know how I could live without you. Don't you ever put me in that position, and I mean not ever! God knows, you've come close a couple of times already, and I'm not going to put up with it. You can go save the world all you want to, but you have to come home safe to me when you're done. Got that?"

Sam grinned back the laughter, and it even infected Ken, who was sitting on the other bed. "I got it," Sam said, "don't worry, Baby. Listen, we're just about to get on the road. I'll give you a call later this afternoon, and let you know what's going on then. I love you, Babe."

"Okay. I love you, too. I'll talk to you then, Baby."

Sam cut off the call, and looked over at Ken. "I'm not sure what was so funny," he said, "because when that girl says she wants me home safe, she isn't kidding. Trust me on this, I know."

Ken nodded. "Then, you trust me on this. I can't make any promises, but I'm going to do my best to make sure you do get home safe to her. You're a very lucky man, Sam Prichard, to have someone who loves you that much. That's not a luxury I could ever afford, you know. I never got to know my own daughter, so I'm going to do everything I can to make sure you get back home to yours. Maybe that'll buy me a little bit of good karma, you think? God knows I could use it!" He got up off the bed, and picked up the small bag he had brought into the room with him. "You ready? We've still got about a hundred miles to go, but I think we should stretch that a bit, and take a longer way into the city. We know Chandler has people watching for us, and I'd just as soon not give them the chance to collect whatever bounty he's put on our heads. Like it or not, we have a mission, and an awful lot of the world is counting on us pulling it off.

Not just our own country, but others as well; there's an awful lot riding on us stopping this egotistical maniac."

Sam picked up his own gear, and started toward the door. "It just seems to me that somebody like Harry should be able to pick up the phone, call the president and say, 'Excuse me, Mr. President, that there's a lunatic loose in the CIA who wants to bring on the battle of Armageddon. Could you slap him down for us?' That would solve the problem for us, wouldn't it?"

Ken rolled his eyes, and shook his head at Sam. "Okay, have you bothered to take a look at who's in the White House right now? The number one Islamic sympathizer in the entire freaking country is currently living at 1600 Pennsylvania Avenue in DC. How do you think he got there?"

Sam stared at him. "Are you trying to tell me that the President of the United States owes Chandler favors?"

"What I'm telling you is that if you made that phone call you were just talking about, Chandler would hear about it before you managed to put the receiver down. Don't you remember the fuss a while back about just where the president was actually born? How do you think so many things got covered up and whitewashed? At least two federal judges ruled that the evidence showed that the president was not a natural born US citizen, and yet he's still in office. A political campaign can't arrange things like backdated birth certificates and modified school records, but the CIA can. Are you catching on yet?"

Sam looked at him for another moment, then simply turned and walked out the door. When Ken followed, he found Sam shoving his bag behind the seat in the Corvette, so he did the same with his own and then got into the passenger seat and shut the door. Sam slid in behind the wheel, put the key in the ignition and cranked the big engine up. He put the shifter in reverse, eased out the clutch and backed away from the room, then shifted into first and headed for the highway.

There was a small restaurant near the exit, and Sam pointed. "Want some breakfast?" he asked.

Ken nodded. "You know what? That sounds like a good idea. After all, it could be our last meal. We might as well enjoy it, right?"

Sam didn't answer, but downshifted and turned the car to enter the parking lot. He pulled up beside the building, shut it down and set the parking brake before getting out.

The two of them walked in and chose a booth near the window, where Sam could keep an eye on the car and Ken could watch for the death squad. They both ordered coffee from the bored waitress, and they both ordered the steak and eggs that was the house specialty, and waited without talking until their orders arrived. The food was surprisingly good, and Sam grunted in appreciation.

"Well," he said, "at least, if it turns out to be our last

meal, it was a good one."

Ken grinned at him and nodded once. "It's actually better than I expected it to be," he said. "Pretty darn tasty, to be honest. I've eaten in so many restaurants in so many places around the world, that sometimes I forget what a decent meal tastes like. This certainly isn't bad."

They finished eating, and walked back out to the Corvette. They were just about to open the doors when a car pulled into the parking lot in a hurry, its tires squealing, and four men jumped out. Sam and Ken reacted almost as one, spinning to face the car and drawing their weapons in a single movement.

The four men who had exited the car suddenly froze, seeing a pair of automatic pistols pointed at them. None of them was armed, and the panic in their faces told the two instantly that they were just some guys in a hurry to get breakfast, and not a group of CIA assassins. Both men holstered their weapons, muttered apologies and got into the car, and Sam quickly drove them away. In the rear view mirror, he could see the four men staring at them and for the first time cursed the fact that his car was rare and noticeable.

"Well, we scared those poor guys half to death," he said. "Think that will lead Chandler's people to us, somehow?"

"No doubt about it," Ken replied. "Those boys will be calling the police, and anything to do with you or me is undoubtedly flagged to get Chandler's attention. If they got your tag number, then he'll know we were here in fifteen minutes. Maybe less. I think you'd better take the next exit, and start driving randomly for a while. They're going to be expecting us to be heading for DC, and of course we are, but that doesn't mean we can't take a detour to throw them off our trail."

Sam nodded, and when the next exit appeared he eased up the ramp. It ended at a road that seemed to be in the middle of nowhere, a two-lane blacktop that only went north or south. Sam took a left and headed north, and because they seemed to be out in the boondocks, he opened up the big engine and raced the car up the road at more than a hundred miles an hour. When he saw a town approaching a few miles up the road, he dropped his speed back to the limit.

The road he was on met a state highway in the middle of town, so Sam took another left, actually heading away from their destination. Once they got out of town, he opened the car up again, and only minutes later came upon another highway headed north again. He took that turn, as well, and followed that road for about twenty miles before turning east once more.

"There aren't enough roads in this part of the country for me to throw them off for long," he said, "but maybe that gave us a little bit of an edge. This road should take us close to where we're going, and we can figure out the last bit of the trip when we get into the city." He glanced over at Ken, who simply nodded. "So how are we going to get close to this guy if I can ask? I mean, you do have a plan, right?"

"I've got several," Ken said, "and which one we use depends on what's going wrong at the moment. One thing you can be certain of, no matter how we try to plan, Chandler is going to be one step ahead of us. You see, he knows exactly what we are out to do, which is put a bullet in his brain. He'll be thinking through how he would plan to do that if he were in our shoes, so whatever plan we come up with, he will have already thought out. Now, that means that we better have more than one plan, so when one starts to go wrong we can simply switch to another. Make sense?"

Sam rolled his eyes. "It makes so much sense that it actually scares me," he said. "Somehow, I think I'd be happier if I didn't understand you at all. But what I was really trying to ask, is what our first step should be when we get to the city. Can you tell me?"

"Yep," Ken said. "Our first step is to stay alive. If I had to guess, I'd say there are probably two dozen armed men trying to track us down right now, and half of them are in that city keeping their eyes on the most likely approaches they think we would use. The mistake they're making, however, is in thinking that we're going to try to get to Chandler in his office. Now, granted, I've done some incredible things in my career, but I'm not Tom Cruise, and this isn't *Mission: Impossible.* Maybe in the movies, some super spook could slip right into CIA headquarters, but I don't see it happening in real life, and certainly not with two guys whose faces have targets painted on them. No, what we will have to do is draw Chandler out, away from his office and away from his goons. In order to do that, we've got to have something he wants. And it will have to be something he wants badly enough to risk his life to get it."

Sam's eyebrows went up a notch. "And we've got something he wants that bad?"

Ken smiled at him. "We don't," he said, "but you do."

Another notch. "I do? Care to enlighten me on that?"

"Sure," Ken said. "You have my head. And you're willing to serve it to Chandler on a platter!"

2

Ron Thomas tapped on his boss's door and waited until he heard the old man inside call out for him to enter. One thing you never did was walk in on Harry Winslow without his consent; those who did so had a tendency to end up dead.

"Ron," the old fellow said in his southern drawl, "what might you have for me this morning?"

"We got an ID on one of the bodies from your house," Ron said without preamble. "Somebody didn't do a good enough job of scrubbing his past, and we got a hit on his fingerprints. He's an ex-Marine named Robert Hawthorne. He was recon, with an impressive body count in Afghanistan. No family, no living relatives, and just the kind of guy the company likes to go after for wet work."

"And have you anything that ties him to Grayson Chandler? Any kind of link at all? Knowing the name of

a man I just killed doesn't help me unless I can link him
to the bastard who sent him after me."

Ron shook his head. "I've got Kathy working on it,
and Jeff is digging into it as well, but so far there's
nothing. That's why they use guys like him, so there
won't be any connections. Unless somebody slipped up
even worse than they did in not clearing his prints out of
all the computers, we're not going to find anything to
connect him to Chandler. Harry, you know that, so don't
get mad at me for not being able to do what can't be
done."

Harry chuckled. "Gotta keep my top man on his
toes," he said. "How do you think I learned enough to get
where I am today? It was from an old scoundrel just like
me. I'm just passing on the same kind of training I
received. One day you'll thank me."

Ron grinned and nodded. "Probably," he said.
"Anything I can do for you this morning?"

Harry finally looked up at him. "Yes," he said. "Send
Eduardo out for some doughnuts, but not the ones we
usually get. There's got to be someplace in this city we
haven't already gone, so pick one of those. And have
somebody bring me another cup of coffee, mine's just
about empty."

Ron rolled his eyes. "Well, there's no sense in that,
now, is there? I'll get you a cup, be right back." He
turned and walked out of the office, and went to the
break room they had set up when they moved into the

new building. He took down one of the big Styrofoam cups that were stacked on the counter, and filled it with coffee from the urn that was marked "Battery Acid." Only he and Harry could stand to drink the coffee out of that one, because it was so strong that if they left the spoon in it for a couple of days, it would dissolve. At least, that was the rumor.

He carried the cup back to Harry's office and knocked on the door again. Even if you were bringing a gift, you still didn't walk in on Harry unannounced. Harry told him to come in, and he set the cup on the edge of Harry's desk. The old man opened the door without looking, reached in and took out what looked like a stirring stick which he stuck into the coffee. He held it there for a couple of seconds, then pulled it out and looked at the end. It was still white, so he dropped it into the trashcan, then picked up the cup and took a sip.

"Good stuff," he said. Ron knew that was his dismissal, so he turned and left the office again. He stopped at the security room and asked Eduardo to go and get the doughnuts. "Harry's a little paranoid again," he said, "what with Chandler after him, so run over into Aurora. I think there's a couple of places on the main drag there, so get a couple dozen regular glazed, and then a couple dozen assorted. That ought to cover us." He reached into a pocket and counted off a couple of twenties, which he gave to Eduardo. "Don't forget to bring me a receipt."

"No problem, chief," the big Hispanic said. "You want

23

anything else while I'm out?"

Ron shook his head and headed back to his own office. This place was a far cry from the little two-man operation he'd run for the last couple of years, while Harry was in deep cover as a drug lord. Only a few of the local cops had ever even heard of him, which only went to show how well Ron and his assistant, Jeff, had done their jobs. Ron had enjoyed seeing the looks on the faces of those cops when it was revealed that Harry was the Homeland Security agent who had been instrumental in thwarting the most devastating terror attack our country had ever known. Now that Harry was running the HS office in Denver, he had a natural budget to work with, a real staff that included genuine agents and intelligence analysts, and a very nice office building only a stone's throw from the state capital. *It was nice to feel like you were finally getting the respect you deserved*, Ron mused.

He sat down at his desk, turned to the computer monitor and began scrolling through the reports his people were constantly posting to their internal server. Ron was something of a legend in the agency, already, because he always seemed to be right on top of whatever his people were doing. So far, no one above him had caught on to the fact that he required all of his analysts to keep notes on the computer of everything they read, did, or even thought about the information that came through their hands. What kind of supervisor would he be, he wondered, if he hadn't left himself a way to look at those notes?

What it boiled down to was that he was basically looking over all of their shoulders at the same time, so that as soon as one of them made an observation, it was available for him to read on his monitor. It was an incredibly simple system, but it worked. When he had shown it to Harry, the old man had patted him on the shoulder and said, "Thank God you're on our side."

"What's that supposed to mean?" Ron asked him, and Harry smiled.

"It just occurs to me that if Hitler had had this little system of yours, he would have seen all of his strengths and weaknesses long before the allies had a chance to use them against him. I suspect that, had that been the case, we'd probably all be speaking German about now." The old man had simply turned and walked away without another word, and Ron wondered if he had just been handed a compliment or an insult. He never did figure out for sure which one it was.

Islamabad — something going on with Achmed Tubal's group there. Sent request for clarification.

David Akbar in London is meeting with investors from Syria later this week. He's looking for funding for some new weapon designs; we better keep an eye on this.

Denver international, security officers there say there's a discrepancy in the number of passengers that have passed through the airport in the last forty-eight hours. Flight records versus debarkation counts are showing that eight people got off of flights that they never bought tickets for. Three flights involved, originating from Los Angeles, Chicago and Miami. Three extra people on each of the first two, and two on the one from Miami. Somehow they all boarded the flights without passes, and were ignored in the pre-takeoff count. The flight attendants are being flagged for questioning. This sounds a lot like the way we get people into other countries, by bribing or seducing the flight attendants into ignoring our people in the pre-flights. Considering the current uproar with people trying to kill the old man, I'm going to recommend sending our own people out to sit in on those interviews.

That last entry had come from Ginger Martin, one of the girls that Ron himself had recruited. She had been busted by the FBI a few months before, when they determined that she was planning some of the most daring daylight bank robberies in recent history. She had a knack for spotting patterns in security personnel behavior, and could exploit those patterns to create plans that allowed a crew to get into and out of bank vaults without being seen except on video, and then only when it was too late. That crew had been run by her uncle, who had somehow realized just how talented she was with computers and had been forcing her to help him plan these crimes.

Under the circumstances, Ron had been able, with Harry's help, to get her charges dismissed on the condition that she work for HS for at least five years. Her security clearances were limited, and she was on twenty-four-hour monitoring, which meant that all of her cell phone conversations were recorded and analyzed, and there were cameras and microphones hidden in her car and her apartment. Because of the way she had come to work for the government, she was considered a high risk, and so every move she made was under scrutiny. Fortunately, she didn't know that, so she was able to go on with a fairly normal life. As long as she didn't end up dating the wrong person, or offer to sell information to someone, she'd probably be fine.

She tapped on his door at that moment, and he looked up and motioned for her to come in. Unlike Harry's office, his was surrounded by glass. Ginger stepped inside and closed the door behind her, then took the chair in front of his desk.

"What's up, girl?" Ron asked. He was fairly sure he knew, but he wanted to hear her say it.

"Something funny out of the airport," she said. "According to their security office, we've had eight invisible men fly in on flights in the last couple of days. I bet a couple of them would be the ones Harry took out, but that means there are six more wandering around town. My guess is that some of them are probably looking for the old man, wouldn't you think? They put out an order for the flight attendants to be questioned about this, and I think we should send someone out to sit in on the interview."

Ron looked at her for a moment. "Who would you send, if it were up to you?" He asked.

"If it were up to me, I'd send me, of course. I think I'd spot a lie faster than anyone else, and I'm certain that I could figure out exactly how they pulled this off. In my mind, there's only one of three answers. Bribery, drugs or seduction."

Ron cocked his head to the right, and grinned. "You're forgetting blackmail," he said. "A threat of some unbearable consequence can make people do things they never do under normal circumstances."

Ginger shook her head. "No I'm not," she said, "because extortion is nothing but another form of bribery. You can bribe someone by offering them something they want, or with the opportunity to avoid something they would consider unpleasant. Either way, they make the choice that they consider most beneficial to themselves. It's still bribery, no matter how you look at it."

Ron considered what she had said for a moment, and then nodded. "You're right, of course," he said. "Not very many people would be capable of seeing it that way, but you did. I'm impressed. When is the interview scheduled?"

"Tomorrow morning, 10 am. They're going to have all of the flight attendants gathered up together, and interview them one at a time. They had to reshuffle some of their schedules to get them all back to Denver, but their security office was pretty adamant about it."

"Yeah, I would be, too. Okay, you're on this. I'll put in an order for you to sit in on the interview, and to record it with both video and audio. You may want to go back over it later, so that way you can. Oh, and incidentally, good work."

Ginger grinned, and Ron thought he saw a hint of a blush, as well. It was really too bad that the agency didn't allow dating amongst its employees, because he suspected that she kind of liked him. Oh well, rules were rules. Besides, he sort of had a girlfriend. At least, when she wasn't mad at him for missing dates or being ridiculously late.

The morning dragged on, with good points and bad ones. Eduardo got back with the doughnuts, which was always a high point around the office, but then one of the secretaries got a call that her daughter had gotten sick at school. The lady wasn't essential to their operations, so Ron told her to go ahead and leave.

Of course, he checked out the situation to make sure that the child's illness wasn't part of some ruse by their current enemies. Even a secretary, under the right circumstances, can be turned into a spy or an assassin. It had happened, many times in the past, and would undoubtedly happen again in the future. Ron just wasn't going to have it happen on his watch.

His phone rang suddenly, and he jumped. The phone on his desk didn't ring very often, and when it did, it usually wasn't good news. He picked up the receiver. "Ron Thomas," he said.

"Well, Ron, Boy," Harry said, "I knew who I was calling, but thank you for telling me that I got through to the right person. I'm just checking in, have we got anything new?"

Ron shook his head, even though he knew Harry couldn't see him. "Afraid not," he said. "The only thing of any interest is something we basically already knew, that we've got some spooks coming in through the airport. I've got Ginger going out to sit in on the interview with the flight attendants tomorrow, just so we have our own idea of what's going on there. Besides the two you killed, there are six more floating around the city, and I've already stepped up our security watch around the building. Anybody shows up here snooping around, we'll spot them. I told the boys we want them alive, not dead. Of course, you know how that goes; they're usually under orders not to be taken alive."

He could hear Harry sigh through the phone. "Fine, fine," Harry said. "If you hear anything new on Sam, I want to know about it instantly. Sending him with Ken Long into DC is a lot like when Daniel got tossed into the lion's den. I'm afraid that boy had better be praying pretty hard, if he has any hope of getting out of this one alive."

"Harry, a couple months ago I would've agreed with you," Ron said. "The thing is, Sam Prichard is probably the most natural agent either one of us has ever seen, and considering what an old fart you are, that's saying something big. If anybody can pull this off, it will be those two. The real question in my mind is how you're going to keep Uncle Sam from deciding to burn them both, and all of us, when it's over. Got that figured out yet?"

Harry chuckled, and Ron felt the shiver that always ran down his spine when that happened. "Son, what you need to remember is that, next to Chandler, I probably know where more bodies are buried than just about anyone else in government service. There aren't too many people who will risk pissing me off if they can avoid it. That will be especially true once Mr. Chandler is not around to try to protect them. If our boys get the job done, I'm not worried about the repercussions. On the other hand, if they don't, I strongly suspect that we should start studying up on our Sunday school lessons."

It was Ron's turn to laugh, but it felt sour to him. "Harry, do you really believe there's any room for us in Heaven? After the things we've done?"

"Why, Ron, why would you ask such a question? Even Judas Iscariot could have been forgiven, so that means there's hope for an old codger like me. I can honestly say that almost everyone I ever killed not only had it coming, but benefited our country by making their exit. What about you? I don't think you've ever killed anyone yet, have you?"

"Harry," Ron said, "haven't you ever heard of the Fifth Amendment? I'll just hope you're right, be sure to say my prayers at bedtime. I'll let you know if I hear anything."

"You do that, Son, on both counts." The line went dead instantly.

Ron shook his head. Harry was one of the strangest old men he'd ever known, and he often wondered what it would have been like to have known him when he was younger. From the stories he heard, Harry was probably America's answer to that famous British super spy. Ron wondered what might've happened if Harry Winslow had run into James Bond. It certainly would've been a battle of dinosaurs, because each of them was about as outdated as a T-Rex.

Ron went back to reading his notes, but there was nothing of any great importance coming through them. He fought off the temptation to call Sam, knowing that Harry would call him when he got impatient enough. Something was definitely going to go down in DC within the next day or so, and it was quite possible that the whole world would be different when the sun came up afterward. If Chandler managed to come out on top, it would be highly doubtful that anyone would ever get another chance to take him out. He had so many powerful friends that it wasn't likely he'd ever be vulnerable again.

* * * * *

Harry was thinking similar things, but from his perspective, this mission was something that had been coming for a while. No, he hadn't known what Chandler was up to until Ken Long had been thrown into their laps, but there was a part of Harry that always believed that some Divine Providence had been directing the events of his life for many years. To him, that Providence was what he thought of as God, and he wasn't above whispering a prayer now and then.

On that particular day, considering the mission and all that was riding on it, Harry had reached the conclusion that God had thrust Sam Prichard into his life. Like Ron, Harry had never seen a man who was better suited to the work of a secret agent then Sam was, but he had become so fond of the young man that it broke his heart to see him forced to do things that so violated his own moral codes. Some recruiter at some college had certainly missed out failing to find Sam Prichard and sign him up for the CIA, or even the FBI. Their loss, however, was Harry's gain, because even when most of Capitol Hill thought Harry was safely out to pasture, he had suddenly discovered the young man who had already saved the country twice. Sam's accomplishments had been the foundation upon which Harry's superiors had been forced to build his new position, establishing a full Homeland Security office in Denver, to replace the satellite office Harry had been running secretly for almost a decade.

There was no more secrecy; Harry Winslow was now

known as Homeland Security's man, and half of Capitol Hill was frightened. As old as Harry was, he knew things going back as far as the seventies, things that everyone in DC wanted to keep buried as deeply as possible. It wasn't even necessary to know what those secrets were, to be aware that if Harry ever decided to let go of all he knew, heads were certain to roll, and they would be rolling right down Pennsylvania Avenue.

Harry thought it was funny. While he did have his own version of the dead man's stash – a large batch of files that would be released to various members of the press if anything happened to Harry – he had enough safeguards on it that there was little risk that anyone would ever see any of those files. Instead of having it set up so that they would be automatically released if he failed to login to some secret server, he had spent a lot of money having a program written so it would simply scan various news sites looking for a death announcement about him, and then check certain other websites that were less public, looking for cues that would say whether his death was natural or not. If it was death by natural causes, the files would instantly be shredded and destroyed; if not, then an awful lot of reporters were going to get emails that would keep them up and awake for several nights.

Harry didn't want to ruin anybody's reputation, but he did want to live as long as possible. A dead man's stash was simply a new form of life insurance, and it was fairly common in the political and intelligence communities. By now, Harry was sure that Ron had one of his own, and he made a note to ask. If the boy didn't have one, it was time he got one set up. He knew where a few bodies had ended up, already, which made him a liability to some people.

A light blinked on his phone, telling him that someone was trying to reach him. He picked up the receiver. "Yes?"

"Mr. Winslow? You've got a call coming in from New York; do you want to take it? It's — it's her."

Harry smiled. "Well, of course I'll take it," he said. "Put 'er through." He waited for a moment as the phone made clicks and beeps, and then he heard that famous voice.

"Harry? Are you there?"

"Why, Sandra," Harry said. "What a surprise. What can I do for you, my dear?"

"Harry, you're no fool. You know exactly why I'm calling you. I got a call from our dear friend Grayson, and he's asked me to try to get you off his back. I don't need to remind you, do I, that I have certain information regarding your last trip to Europe that I'm pretty sure you don't want to get out?"

Harry burst out laughing. "If you are referring to my dalliance with a certain member of the British royalty, I can assure you that I could care less who found out about that! In the first place, who would believe it? And in the second, who cares? Those people do more stupid stuff in a half hour than our Hollywood stars can do in six weeks. And while we're on the subject of who knows what about who, do you really want to go there? Have you forgotten who was standing in the room with a certain First Lady, when she overruled her husband and demanded that a church full of men, women and children be burned to the ground? Do you honestly think I didn't manage to get copies of the monitoring tapes from that office? Don't threaten me, darlin', unless you're ready to play in the big leagues. I like you, kiddo, I really do, but I could destroy you in a matter of seconds, and you know it. Don't ever make me do it, okay? I'd really hate it."

The lady on the other end of the line laughed, a hearty laugh that said she'd gotten exactly the response she had been expecting. "Trust me, you old buzzard, I never will. I promised Grayson that I would call you, and I did. Can I call him back and tell him you said you'd consider it?"

"You can if you want to lie," Harry said. "The only thing I'm going to consider is what dance I plan to do on his grave. Things have gone too far, and whether you believe his take on the prophecies, or the Bible's, either way, things are coming to a head. I don't know about you, my dear, but I want to be on the winning side. Now, Chandler is putting all his chips on some weird Mesopotamian God that he thinks can whip all the rest of them. I've read up on that one, that *Shamash*, and what bothers me is that I can't find any record of his prophecies that have already come true. On the other hand, a nice, long read through the Good Book will show you hundreds of prophecies that can be proven to have come true already. My favorite is how Daniel was able to predict that Alexander the Great would attempt to invade Israel hundreds of years before he was born. When he showed up to begin that invasion, the Jewish high priest simply showed him the prophecy which so obviously pointed to him, and he was so blown away by it that he not only didn't invade, he went into the Jewish temple and made a sacrifice to the God Jehovah. Pretty amazing that the prophecies could be so detailed, isn't it? I think I'm going to stick on the side of the God who can pull off a coup like that. That's what you can tell Chandler, and you can tell him also that I think it's disgusting he's hiding behind a girl. You have a great day, my dear, okay? We'll talk later." He hung up without even saying goodbye.

Harry leaned back in his chair and stared up at the ceiling. If Chandler was reaching out that far, then he was more worried than he was admitting. There was something that Harry was missing, and he knew it. Now all he had to do was figure out what it was.

For some reason, Chandler was getting scared. He was calling in favors that he should've saved for once he got his plans in motion, and that told Harry that he was worried about what Sam and Ken were likely to do. Somehow, he had come to the conclusion that there was a chance he was going to lose this gambit. What could be making him nervous? That was what Harry had to figure out.

He sat forward again, and picked up his cell phone. He tapped the icon for Sam and held the instrument to his ear. Sam answered on the second ring, and Harry smiled.

"Sam, Boy, how are you, Son?"

"Still on the road, Harry, how's it going on your end?"

"Sam, I'm not sure. I just got a call from somebody big enough that it tells me Chandler is getting nervous. He's rattling chains he shouldn't be rattling, not yet. He should be saving some of these people for when he really needs them, with the program he's put in the motion. I'm not sure what's got him scared, but something does. For some reason, he thinks you just might get to him. Any clue what could bring that about?"

"Not yet, Harry. Ken's got a plan, but we haven't done anything about implementing it yet. You got any ideas?"

Harry scowled. "Nothing, nothing at all. I don't know what's got him rattled, but we need to figure it out, so we can use it against him. Anything that makes him nervous can strengthen our position, so if we can figure out what it is, it improves the odds of our success. Keep your thinking caps on, and let me know if you come up with anything."

"We will, Harry. Ken is looking at me with his eyes wide, so I don't think he knows any more than I do. On the other hand, we're only about an hour out of the city now, and we're coming in through some residential areas. Wish us luck."

"You know I do," Harry said, and then he hung up again. In the Corvette that was nearly seventeen hundred miles away, Sam looked over at Ken and muttered something about Harry lacking in social skills.

Harry wasn't worried about being sociable; he was worried about how to keep his country and its sovereignty intact. Globalization would come, that he knew, but that didn't mean he was looking forward to it. As long as there was breath in his body, he knew he would fight the concept and do all he could to delay it or stop it if that were in his power. That was the whole reason behind the mission his boys were on right now, and the fact that Chandler was nervous was giving him just a little touch of hope.

3

"It's called the Matomic building," Ken said. "It was actually built not long after World War II, by an Italian immigrant named Jerry Miaitico. Because we had just taken out Hiroshima and Nagasaki not long before, Jerry wanted this building to be one that could withstand an atomic attack so he built it with an incredible amount of steel girders. That's how it got its name: M for Miaitico, plus the word atomic, equals Matomic. Once it was built, Jerry leased it to the federal government. Its very first tenant was an organization that was considered top-secret at the time, the Atomic Energy Commission. Ironic wasn't it?"

Sam grinned. "Sort of fitting, if you ask me."

"Yeah, it was. There were a lot of little diversions along the way, but eventually the government set out to force Jerry to sell them the building. They even tried to take it under eminent domain, but he found himself an incredibly bright lawyer by the name of Herschel Shanks, and Shanks actually wrote a brief that beat the government at its own game. That didn't happen often, but in this case it worked out well. Jerry's daughters inherited the building when he passed away, and they eventually sold it to the government for an incredible fortune. Three floors of that eleven-story monstrosity ended up dedicated to the CIA. Now, mind you, this was before the CIA settled in Langley. That's where their headquarters is now, but they still maintain their offices in the Matomic building, and since it's only a block from the White House, that's where Chandler's senior Islamic desk is located. I think the reasoning is because, if he comes up with something critical in the way of a warning about impending terrorist activity, and for any reason it's considered too sensitive for the extremely secure phone lines in DC, well, then he can just take off and jog down the street to brief the president. Don't look at me like that, I know how stupid that sounds, but that's exactly how stupid Washington politics can be."

Sam held up his hands as if to ward off his comment. "Hey, I'm just along for the ride, remember?"

"Ride, my aunt Mabel," Ken said. "You're driving, remember? Okay, turn right at the next light. We don't want to get too 'close before we park this thing. If we had half a lick of sense, we'd have hidden it somewhere and stolen us a station wagon. Something that wouldn't stand out like a sore thumb, anyway. You and your hot rods!"

Sam made the turn and then pointed. "All day

parking, ten dollars. Looks like a good place to leave the Corvette, don't you think?"

Ken nodded. "It'll do," he said. "You do have comprehensive insurance on this thing, right? I mean, when it gets stolen, somebody's gonna send you a nice big check, right?"

Sam pulled into the parking lot and chose an empty spot. "I hope you're being a smart Alec," he said, "but yeah, I've got theft insurance. Just hope I never have to file the claim. I've got years of work invested in this car. I'm not sure I've got it in me to do all that again."

Ken was flipping through several debit cards that he'd taken from a pocket, and passed one to Sam. "Swipe this one to pay for the parking," he said. "It will lead back to either of us, so hopefully Chandler won't know the Corvette is here for at least a few hours. That ought to give us a little bit of a head start on them, a chance to find a position where we can spot the killers coming. Let's go, out of the car. We can't afford to sit in one spot for more than a few minutes, not in the city."

Sam got out, leaving his bag behind the seat, and he noticed that Ken did the same. That almost made him nervous, because it implied that they wouldn't be needing a change of clothes. As far as Sam was concerned, the only ones who didn't need a change of clothes were dead men.

He swiped the card Ken had given him in the machine, punched in the number of the parking space he had taken and waited for a moment while it printed a receipt. The system was completely automated, so that when he went to leave, he would hold the receipt up to a reader on the exit gate. The reader would scan a bar code, and decide whether Sam was paid up, or owed more money. If he was within the time allowed for the all day, ten-dollar fee, then the gate would open and let him go. If not, it would demand more money before opening.

"They get you coming and going," Ken said. "This city has more ways to fleece money out of you than anyplace else I've ever been in the entire world. Doesn't matter how tight you hold onto your wallet, trust me, somebody here will get money out of it."

Sam grinned at him. "That wasn't my money they just got, it was yours."

"No, it wasn't," Ken said, grinning back. "That card was a phony, backed up by some fictitious bank account somewhere in New Jersey. Whenever I'm sent out on a mission, I end up with some of those. A few years ago, I figured out that they don't ever cancel them once I'm done, so I just started holding onto them. I mean, you never know when you might need an extra fifty bucks or so, right? Some of the ones I've got only have a couple hundred dollars on them, and some of them have a few thousand. It's just nice to have something to fall back on."

Sam blinked. "Yeah, I'll bet it is. I take it those are expense accounts?"

"Yeah, something like that. Whoever I'm working for gives me one to use for the expenses of the mission, I'm assuming so that they can keep track of where I'm at and what I'm doing. When the mission is over, they tend to forget about those little accounts, so I just hang onto the cards for emergencies. Like having something put back for a rainy day, you know? I've been living off of them for the last two years, now. Ever since I went off the reservation and onto this mission."

They had parked near the corner of I Street and twentieth, and were walking in the general direction of H Street. Chandler's office was in the building there, and while they didn't want to get too close, they needed to be closer than they already were.

As Ken had suggested, the plan was to try to use him as bait. They had to find a way to get Chandler alone, and that wasn't going to be easy to do. The only thing that he might want badly enough to risk coming out of his secure location would be the chance to shut Ken down for good.

Of course, that meant convincing him that Sam was willing to turn on Ken and hand him over. In order to do that, Sam would have to do the best acting he'd ever done, convincing Chandler that all he wanted was the chance to go home and live a normal life with his family. If it worked, Chandler would meet with them and hopefully, they would get the chance to take a shot that would put an end to his power in the political world.

"Okay," Sam said, "now, assume something goes wrong and he just decides to put a bullet in each of our heads. We'll be dead, and he just rides off into the sunset, right?"

"We're not going to make it that easy for him," Ken said. "He has a life here, he's well known. We meet in a public place and he can't risk taking a shot at us. Someone would whip out a cell phone, and he'd be on YouTube ten minutes later. He can't take that chance." He grinned. "I, on the other hand, am a spook. They can post me on the Internet all they want to, and if anyone can identify me, more power to them. All it will do is add to the mystique of my reputation. I can assure you, it wouldn't be the first time that I had been caught on camera in the middle of an assassination. I've probably already starred in a few videos, that doesn't mean anything to me."

"But do you really think he'll be alone? If it were me, I'd have a half-dozen people hiding in the crowd, so that all I had to do was point the finger and stand back and watch while we got blown away. We know he has goons; why wouldn't he bring several with him?"

"You misunderstand me; I'm assuming that he will. Hopefully, I can spot them before they spot us. We'll need to take them out, first, before we can get close enough to Chandler to do the job." He reached into a pocket and pulled out what looked like a hearing aid. He handed it to Sam and pointed at his ear. "Put that on," he said. "Tuck that little wire inside your ear, it's got the speaker on it. I've got one, too, they're like little telephones. The microphone is super sensitive, and can pick up what you say, even if you whisper. Once we get the meeting set up, we'll turn these on so that we can work together on taking out his backup. Just remember, once you've identified one of them, you can't hesitate. It has to be a shot and it has to be fatal. You can't capture these guys, and you can't turn them. All you can do is kill them."

"I understand," Sam said, and he reached back under his jacket and withdrew a pistol from the waistband of his pants. It was smaller than his Glock, a thirty-two caliber automatic with a silencer, one that Harry had given him once before when he was warned he might have to shoot first, and ask questions later. "I'm ready, and I'll do what I have to do." He slipped the little pistol back into hiding.

Ken smiled and patted him on the shoulder. "I don't doubt your courage, Sam," he said. "You've got bigger *cojones* than just about anyone I've ever known. You've already taken on things that even I would've hesitated to tackle. I'm not a bit worried about your courage, but that doesn't mean that you can overcome a lifetime of conditioning that says you can't just walk up and shoot someone through the head. Not too many people can do that, not without going through a little bit of self-recrimination. The trouble is, you won't have time to argue with yourself about whether you are doing the right thing. You have to take the shot, take it quickly and make sure it's right between the eyes."

Sam stopped walking and turned to face him. "Look, Ken, I get it," he said. "And just between you and me, it won't be the first time that I've gone into something knowing I was going to kill someone. That whole terrorist nuke thing at Hoover dam? Trust me, I had every intention of killing that kid. Not only did he have a nuclear bomb that he was planning to use against my country, but he had murdered my best friend and former partner. He bought himself a death sentence the minute he pulled that trigger." He turned and started walking again, and Ken grinned as he followed.

"Like I said, Sam, I wasn't worried about your courage. Now I'm less worried, and more sure we're going to find some way to pull this off."

They kept walking for a couple of blocks, and then turned left. Sam noticed two men suddenly paying attention to them as they turned the corner, and he caught Ken's eye. "You see them?" he asked.

Ken nodded. "Yeah, I did. One of them seems to be talking to his wrist, so he's telling someone up ahead that we're coming in their direction. Are you ready?"

"Ready as I'm ever going to be," Sam said. "I see two up ahead who seem to be looking this direction, as if they're expecting to spot someone." He turned and glanced over his shoulder. "And those two back there are following us, so I'm guessing were about to be squeezed in the middle. This is the part where you pull one of your magic tricks out of your little black bag, right?"

"Something like that," Ken said. "How accurate is that little gun of yours? Say, at thirty feet?"

"Pretty accurate," Sam said, "and we're about to find out, anyway. The two had have just been joined by a third, so we've got five altogether. Two behind and three ahead. How do you want to play this?"

"Well, the street's pretty crowded, so they're not gonna start shooting unless they can get us in the open, away from other people. The longer we can stay bunched up with all these other sheep, the longer they're going to delay taking action. They're following protocol, not firing into crowds; luckily, we don't have that disadvantage. The moment, and I mean the very moment, that you're confident you can fire three shots and take three down, you draw and fire. While you're doing that, I'm going to take out the two behind us. You get the ones in front because you can keep them in sight, I'll take the ones in back because I've got years of experience at rapid target identification. Everything is on you, when you fire, so will I."

Sam swallowed hard. Ken was right, and he could see the three men who were waiting ahead of them; in a matter of seconds, either all three of them would be dead, or Sam would be. He kept walking, trying his best to look unconcerned, until he was close enough that he was sure he could hit all three targets. He knew that it had to be head shots, there could be no possibility of survival.

Two more steps, then one more, *now!* Sam drew the little thirty-two of his waistband and raised it in one smooth motion. *Pop! Pop, pop!* Three shots, barely making any noise through the silencer, and all three of those men were down. Even as he was firing, he heard the two louder booms from Ken's gun as he shot the two men behind them.

The crowd around them was screaming, some people running while others dropped to the ground. Ken spun and grabbed Sam by the arm, propelling him forward at a run. "Put the gun away," he hissed, and Sam shoved the little pistol back into his waistband as they ran.

They ran past the three men Sam had shot, and turned a corner, suddenly finding themselves in another crowd that didn't seem to be aware of the shootings. They stopped running, then moved into the crowd and through it.

Sam looked at Ken. "I don't get it," he said softly, "your gun wasn't silenced. Couldn't these people hear your shots?"

"They probably did, but gunshots are so common in DC that most people just ignore them unless they're happening right close by. Check it out, we're only about four blocks from the White House, but there's enough street crime and drug activity here that anyone who heard the shots will figure that's what it's about. Nobody would even suspect that it might have to do with political intrigue, even though we are smack in the middle of Intrigue Central. Crazy, isn't it?"

Sam shook his head and kept walking. "What's crazy is that we just killed five people, and I don't even hear a police siren. Nobody's running after us, screaming for us to stop — that's wild, Man." He glanced at his hand, which was trembling slightly, then looked back at Ken. "So, after that, I'm guessing that Chandler knows we're here, wouldn't you think? I'm sure at least one of those guys got word to him through a com link."

Ken shrugged, rubbernecking the area and looking for new threats. "That would be a safe bet," he said. "That means it's time for you to make your call. Look, there's a Starbucks up ahead. The Matomic building is only a couple doors down from there, and that's where his office is. Right now, that's where he'll be. I don't know about you, but I could use a latte."

Sam rolled his eyes, but followed Ken into the coffee shop. He took a seat with his back to a wall, positioned so that he could see every entrance, and waited for Ken to get his latte. When he came back to where Sam was sitting, he handed over a straight coffee, as well.

"Chandler's not going to want to come over here," he said, "he'll want to pick a different spot to meet. What you got to do is make sure that it's somewhere very, very public. Make it - make it the front steps of the Lincoln Memorial. Tell him you'll meet him there in an hour, and that you got me disarmed and restrained."

Sam looked at him for a moment, and then shook his head. "This is crazy, Ken," he said. "We're talking about turning you over to him, without weapons and in handcuffs. He can put a bullet through your head as soon as he's got you in sight."

Ken reached into his pocket and produced a pair of handcuffs that he handed to Sam. "You used a lot of these in your time, right? See anything odd about this pair?"

Sam looked them over. "Looks like a pair of regulation police cuffs, to me." He handed them back. "Why?"

Ken grinned, and put the cuffs on himself. When he had them securely snapped around each wrist, he held them out to Sam. "All good and secure?" Ken asked.

Sam felt the cuffs and nodded. "Yeah, good and tight," he said.

Ken chuckled, and hit the two cuffs against each other. Both of them flew open, and literally dropped from his wrists. Sam's eyes went wide, and Ken laughed. "Houdini specials," he said. "I got these from a magician, a guy who does all those escape acts. He gets put in these, and then he goes into a box or something, but the next thing you know, he's free and standing in the crowd beside you. They're wonderful."

"That's pretty cool," Sam said. "So, I hand you over wearing those, and then as soon as the two of you are out of sight, you pop free and then — then what?"

"If everything goes according to plan, then one well-placed strike with the heel of my hand and Mr. Chandler is no longer a problem. The problem with that is that things never go according to plan, so I'll have to wing it as I go along."

"And what am I supposed to be doing all this time? How am I supposed to know whether you succeed or not?"

"That depends on Chandler. I'm not sure what he'll do about you, he may want you to come along as he takes me in. If he does, then he'll want you unarmed, as well."

Sam shook his head. "I think if I go along with that, we're both dead. Giving up my weapon and letting him have us both strikes me as a very bad idea."

"You're not thinking properly," Ken said. "He'll be alone, so there'll be two of us against the one of him. That increases our chances of success. Remember, this guy is as tough as I am; he's not going to be easy to kill, especially without weapons. Nevertheless, we've got to get the job done, somehow. I'm not dead certain what his next move is, but I can guarantee you that it will put America in a worse position on this whole global stage issue. He's got to be stopped before he can make that next move."

Sam took a sip of his coffee, hissing because it was extremely hot. "Lord, I don't know how these people stay in business; they must burn the lips off of most of their customers." He looked at Ken. "I guess that's part of what's making me so nervous, that we don't know what it is he's doing. How do we know for sure that killing him will put a stop to it?"

"Look at the prophecies," Ken said. "Chandler is trying to bypass some of the things that have to happen. If he can do that, then the globalization he'll be bringing on won't be the real thing, and it's possible that it will mess up the situation so badly that the genuine fulfillment of prophecy could be set back years, maybe even decades. That would be enough of a disaster on its own, but a side effect of his activities is his determination to eliminate organized Christianity. Every prophecy from every other religion makes it plain that in order for their view to come to fruition, Christianity must be destroyed. Now, the most powerful tool Chandler has in his arsenal for attacking and destroying Christianity would be Islamic jihad. If he can orchestrate effective Islamic attacks on Christians in various places around the world, including right here in the United States, then some of the people he's got positioned in other countries will begin to gain power. That power will be thrown behind him, making him even stronger than he already is. Sam, he's got to be stopped. Everything our country stands for, everything it was founded on and built on is literally hanging on the edge of a cliff, ready to be toppled over to its destruction. There are very few of us who even see the danger, and we are all that's standing between life and death."

Sam nodded. "Yeah, yeah, I get it. I just wish I knew more about how this is going to play out. If we had some clue what it is he's really up to, it might even give us a better idea of how to move against him. But if this plan is all we've got, then I guess we have to go for it." He looked at Ken. "Are you ready?"

"I'm ready as I'm going to be," he said. "Let's do it."

Ken handed Sam a cell phone, a number already punched in and simply awaiting activation of the call. Sam looked at it for a long moment, and then pushed the green button and held it to his ear. He heard ringing, and then a tentative answer.

"Hello?"

"My name is Sam Prichard," Sam said. "I think we have business to discuss."

There was a silence on the other end for a moment, and then Sam heard some beeps and whistles. A second later, the voice came back on the phone. "What kind of business might we have between us, Sam Prichard?"

"I have Kenneth Long," Sam said. "And I've come to the conclusion that I don't want to be on your bad side. That sounds to me like there might be a potential arrangement for us to make. We can each get what we want, and come out ahead."

"And what is it you want, Mr. Prichard?"

"To be able to go home to my family, and live a normal life. Maybe some sort of job, something I can do to keep that normal life when the world goes crazy."

"And in return, you're willing to give up Mr. Long?"

"Good Lord," Sam said, "isn't that what I just told you? Look, I've got him disarmed and in handcuffs. I'll hand him over, and then you can do with him as you please. I just want out of this mess."

Again there was a silence, and for a moment Sam thought the connection had been cut. Just when he was about to ask if anyone was there, the voice came back. "What about your pal, Harry? I know that he and I are not on the same team, so why would I assume that I can trust you?"

Sam sighed the phone. "Look, Dude, there's something really weird going on here. I don't know what it's all about, but I've got people screaming at me about Bible prophecies and stuff from Babylon, and I don't know what any of them are smoking. The only thing that sounds like it could be true to me is that the world is about to change, but I've been seeing that coming for a long time. Now, if there's one thing I know about change, it's that you have to know which side of the fence to be on when it happens. What I want is to be on the side that will let me raise my daughter and not be involved in any more of this international crap. As for Ken, all I know about him is that he's some kind of government hit man, so if he gets whacked, I'm not going to lose a lot of sleep over it. Now, can we make a deal? Because if not, then I'll have no choice but to throw back in with Harry and Long, and that's not what I want to do."

"Mr. Prichard, tell me what you've got in mind. When and where do you want to meet, and how do you want to hand him over?"

"One hour from now, just you, alone, on the steps of the Lincoln Memorial. That's a nice public place, don't you think? Ken will be with me, his hands cuffed in front of him and covered with his jacket, and I'll have him covered with a silenced automatic from a few feet away. At this point, he knows I don't have anything to lose. If he tries to run, or cause any commotion, he's dead and he knows it. And incidentally, he thinks I'm turning him over to a Justice Department investigator. I gave him a song and dance about how Justice wants him, and told him that Harry had sold him out. He laughed at me and said that so many people at Justice owe him favors that he'll be back on the street ten minutes after I hand him over."

Sam heard Chandler chuckle. "That's pretty shrewd, Mr. Prichard. It's also probably pretty smart, because if he knew you were bringing him to me, there's a good chance you would end up dead. Very well, one hour from now. I'll come alone, as you requested, and I expect you to do likewise, with the exception of our friend Mr. Long. You give him to me, and I will give you a card with a phone number. That number will always be able to reach me, no matter where I am in the world, and will entitle you to certain favors that will help you to achieve your goal of living a normal life with your family. Those favors might include jobs, ways to avoid problems that others might face, things of that nature. Is that agreeable?"

"That'll work just fine," Sam said. "Like I said, all I want is to go home to my family. If I can call on you now and then when there are problems, that would be cool, but mostly I just want out of this mess."

"I believe we have a deal, Mr. Prichard. I'll meet you on the steps in one hour to make our exchange. Do you know what I look like?"

Sam shook his head in futility, since Chandler couldn't see through the phone. "Nope. Not a clue."

"I'll simplify it for you then. I'll be wearing a red nylon windbreaker and a green baseball cap. The cap says Chemtronix on it. And don't worry, I know exactly what you look like."

"I figured you did, since I've already had to take out five of your people. One hour, then. Don't be late, or I'll be gone. This is a one-shot offer."

"Yes, I'll admit I was surprised that you were able to take them down. On the other hand, they were all fairly new; I should've sent more experienced people after you. If you cross me, I won't make that mistake a second time, I want you to be aware of that."

"I'm not planning to cross anybody, and I don't want to be double crossed, either. I keep telling you, all I want is to get out of this mess. If that's acceptable to you, then you can have Long and I'll go my merry way on home. I've got a wife and little girl waiting for me, and they both made me promise to come home safe. That's all I want to do, keep that promise."

"One hour, Mr. Prichard. See you then." The line went dead.

Sam took out his own phone and punched the icon of Elmer Fudd. Here he answered a moment later.

"Sam, Boy? What's going on?"

"We just set up a meeting with Chandler," Sam said. "Ken will be wearing some trick handcuffs that he can escape from, and the idea is that I'm supposed to let Chandler take him. Our story is that I just want to get out of the whole thing, and that I'm willing to betray him or you or anybody to get what I want. At the moment, I think Chandler is going for it. If he does, I'm probably going to be arrested for murdering him. I'm really hoping you can take care of that, if it happens."

"Son, if you can take him down, I'll get you out of trouble. Just be sure they take you alive, because I'm not real good at bringing people back from the dead." He ended the call without another word. Sam looked at the phone for a moment, then shook his head and put it away.

4

Chandler put down the phone and stared at it for a moment. Not for a single second did he believe that Sam Prichard truly intended to hand over Ken Long, and yet he was quite intrigued by the opportunity to find out what their game was. Prichard was Harry Winslow's man, and had already demonstrated some uncanny abilities for an untrained agent. There was a game afoot, but it wasn't the one they were presenting.

He picked up the phone again and dialed a number that would ring in another office within his section. "Stone? It's Grayson. What kind of eyes do we have on the Lincoln Memorial?"

The young man on the other end of the phone line made a polite chuckle. "There are twenty-two security cameras around that complex," he said. "I have digital access to all of them. What are we looking for?"

"I'm going to be meeting someone there in just a little

while. I want you to be watching, and ready to notify backup if I need it. I also want to be sure we have a record of the meeting."

"Well, I can get video off security cameras. If you want audio, then you're going to have to wear a wire. There are a few microphones around the complex, but it's doubtful you'd be close enough that I could pick up any audio."

"Yes, I understood that. I'm leaving now, I'll stop by your office so you can give me a transmitter. Got one ready?"

"Yep. I've always got a few handy, all charged up and ready to go."

Chandler smiled into the phone. "Good job," he said. "I'll be there in a couple of minutes."

He hung up the phone and rose from behind his desk, slipped on his windbreaker and cap, then walked out past his secretary. She glanced up at him and smiled.

"Going out for a bit," he said. "Hold down the fort for me, will you?"

The woman laughed. "Yeah, sure," she said. "Are you going to be gone long? You got a few people who were hoping to see you this afternoon."

"No, I shouldn't be very long. An hour, maybe a little more. I'll be back by lunch time. Can I bring you anything?"

"No, I'm meeting my husband for lunch. Thanks anyway."

Chandler smiled and walked away, turning down the hall towards the office where Gary Stone handled their electronic communications network. "Electronic communications" was a euphemism for the room where Stone controlled all of the electronic monitoring equipment that allowed him to tap into video and audio all around the city. It was also his electronics workshop, where he and his staff developed all sorts of gadgets that Chandler and his people found useful.

"Okay, Stone, what you got for me?"

Gary Stone looked a lot like the typical movie computer nerd. He stood about five foot eight, and wore thick, horn-rimmed glasses, just like the comedy sidekicks in most of the college movies. He looked like a kid who was always trying to get his grades up, but in truth, he had an IQ that probably rivaled some of the greatest thinkers in the world. Chandler considered him a terrific asset, and a particularly exciting feather in his own cap. He found this kid while he was still tinkering with science fair projects in high school, and recruited him even before his graduation.

"Here you go," the kid said. He handed Chandler a small device, about the size of an old book of matches. "Just stick this in your shirt pocket and I'll be able to hear everything within about ten feet of you. We'll record it all, so if we have to clean up the audio later, we can do that."

Chandler looked it over, and grinned. He slipped it

into his pocket and patted the boy on the shoulder. "Good job," he said once again. "You're going to be on the monitor yourself, right?"

"Yep! When you said we were watching a meeting of yours, I figured you would want me to handle personally. So that's what I'm going to do."

Chandler glanced around the room, noting that several of the people there were sneaking surreptitious glances at him. That didn't surprise him, simply because none of these people would be there if they weren't the curious sort. He waved at them all, causing several to duck down behind their computer monitors in a hurry. That gave him a chuckle, as he turned and walked out the door.

He made one other stop before leaving the building, in the little office that dispatched his agents. The girl on the computer there told him that there were four men within a few minutes of the memorial, and he told her to have them positioned close by as soon as possible. He'd let her know, through Stone, if he needed them. He didn't bother to notify Stone, because he expected the boy to be listening already.

It was less than a mile to the Lincoln Memorial, just down Eighteenth Street, alongside the White House complex. There was no point in trying to drive, since most of the roads were blocked off due to unofficial traffic, and it was a nice day so he decided to simply walk. That would take less time than getting a car and going around the long way to come up to the memorial from the south. He hoped to get there in time to see Long and Prichard arrive, but he guessed they were probably already there and waiting for him.

That was okay. He didn't have any delusions that this meeting would actually result in the end of Ken Long's tenure as the thorn in his side. He didn't know what these guys were up to, but unless they were willing to commit murder right out in the open in broad daylight, he wasn't too worried. Besides, he didn't plan to get close enough for them to make a serious attempt, not unless he was absolutely certain that neither of them was armed. They were playing their game, but he was out to play his own.

* * * * *

Sam and Ken had left the coffee shop immediately after ending the call to Harry, and walked down Eighteenth Street toward the memorial. They had about an eight-minute head start on Chandler; he would be walking the same route in just a few minutes.

"He's going to want to frisk me," Ken said, "so I need to find somewhere to get rid of this Colt."

Sam looked at him. "Just give it to me," he said. "I've still got room in my waistband for one more gun, it won't matter. Besides, we might need it." He reached out and accepted it, then slipped it into the left side of his back waistband. His light jacket hung down over it, concealing both of the weapons he had tucked there. "Worse comes to worst, you can drop those funny cuffs and snatch it out quick. If things go wild, I'm not going to bother with the thirty-two, I'm going for my big Glock. With this guy, I'm more interested in stopping power than stealth."

Ken nodded. "If the shooting starts, just put as many bullets into him as you can. And the more you can put into his head, the happier I'll be. Odds on, he's got some sort of body armor under his clothes. He's known for at least thirty hours that we were coming, so he's as ready as he could possibly be."

"Yeah, and in that case, you know he's got people moving into place on us by now. Do you think we can spot them again, and take them out? Good Lord, Ken, the Lincoln Memorial is going to be pretty crowded with tourists, isn't it? Do we really want to start shooting in a situation like that?"

Ken shrugged. "What you got to get to your head is that the most important thing to think about at this moment is putting a stop to Chandler. That's not just something we want to do, it's what we have to do. That's the mission, and anything else that gets in the way is what we call collateral damage. It sucks, but it happens."

"Okay, well, now you've run up on the part that I can't just wrap my head around. I know we need to stop Chandler, but I can't do it at the cost of innocent lives. If he's got people on scene, we can't open fire in the middle of a crowd of tourists; I'm not saying I won't return fire, but I won't start the shooting."

Ken glanced at him, but kept walking. "Okay, I can live with that, but don't get in the way of what I have to do. I promise you, I will never deliberately let an innocent person get hurt, but if the only shot I've got at Chandler has to be through someone else, then I'm going to take the shot."

Sam didn't say anything, but kept walking alongside. It was only a few moments more before the World War II Memorial came into view, and Ken pointed off to the right. The famous reflecting pool was laid out in front of them, and Sam saw the Lincoln Memorial at its other end.

"That's where we're going," Ken said. "Keep your eyes peeled for potential shooters. Odds on, they're here."

"Oh, gee, and I was hoping you were going to tell me we were all clear. I'm watching, don't worry."

The two of them turned and began walking across the National Mall toward the Lincoln Memorial, following the walking paths around the lake at Constitution Gardens and making their way across the grounds. The path they were on took them past the Vietnam Women's Memorial, and they stopped to admire the statue of a nurse holding a fallen soldier.

"Two men watching us, over by the Vietnam Wall. See them?" Ken asked.

Sam nodded. "I do now," he said. "Think they're his?"

"Too early to tell," Ken said. "Let's just keep an eye on them, see what they do. Come on, let's go on."

They started off again toward the granite building that housed the statue of our sixteenth president. Sam tried not to act like a tourist, but since it was his first visit to DC, he was having trouble not gawking at all of the sights. Ken elbowed him. "Come on, Buddy, hold it together. If we get through this alive, I promise to bring you back and get you a guided tour."

Sam sneered at him. "Don't be a smart ass," he said. "I'm on the ball, I just never saw this stuff before, and if things go wrong here, today, I might never get another chance."

Ken grinned, but it wasn't pleasant. "You actually have a good point," he said. "If Chandler gets his way, this will probably be a UN World Heritage site before long, and then us Americans may not be allowed to come and see it at all!"

"Yeah," Sam said, "so I got to take advantage of it while I can. Who knows if I'll ever get another chance?"

"You won't get one if we're dead," Ken said. "Gawk all you want, just make sure you keep your eyes open for the real threats. Those two back by the wall aren't watching us anymore, so I don't think they were any risk, but I'm sure there are others here that are. Peel those eyes, Man."

They made it to the steps of the Memorial without incident, and Ken preceded Sam up the stairs to get a good look at the giant statue of Abe Lincoln.

"It looks like he had the weight of the world on his

shoulders," Sam said. "I wonder how he'd feel if he knew the kind of thing we're up against, today. Terrorism, nuclear threats from all around the world, racial violence all around the country — I just can't help but wonder what he'd think of what has become of the country he fought so hard to keep together."

Ken shook his head. "I don't know, but don't idolize the man. If you studied your history, you know he wasn't quite the hero he's made out to be today. The entire Civil War was fought not because of slavery, like kids are being taught today, but because the president and the federal government completely disregarded the rights of the states who chose to secede from the union. Thousands of Americans on both sides had to die because Lincoln and his cronies simply threw out the Constitution. Every state has the right to certain levels of self-determination, according to the Constitution; unfortunately, ever since Lincoln's day, the federal government has disregarded those rights. Any attempt by states to run themselves the way they see best is met by threats of withholding federal funding that the states have become dependent on. The national Highway system, the welfare program, so many things that seem commonplace today are federally funded, so if the state decides it doesn't want to play ball the way the feds want, they simply cut off the funding and then that state has to fit all those bills itself. The states don't have that kind of money, because unlike the federal government, they can't create it out of thin air. Better go back and read your history, before you start worrying about what Mr. Lincoln might think of our America, today."

Sam turned and looked at Ken. "Good grief, Man, is there anything about this country that you won't complain about? Seems like no matter what we talk about, you've got to be a downer. No wonder nobody likes you that much."

Ken shrugged. "I face reality, my friend. I suggest you learn to do the same."

Sam shook his head. "We better find a position, and take it now. Remember, you're supposed to be my prisoner, and as far as Chandler knows, I'm keeping a gun pointed at you. Maybe we better make it look good, don't you think?"

Ken nodded towards the front of the building. "Let's go to the bottom of the stairs, and you stay a good five feet away from me. Get your pistol in your hand, but keep it tucked under your jacket and stand so that it's aimed at least loosely in my direction. The idea isn't that you've got me covered every second, but that you've got a weapon you can bring to bear to shoot me quickly if you had to. You watch me, and I'll watch everyone else. If for any reason we get separated, remember that you can communicate with me through the earpiece."

They made their way down the steps, and took a position toward the south end of the building, at the bottom of the stairs. As instructed, Sam stayed about five feet back, and turned so that the Glock in his hand could be pointed quickly in Ken's direction. Ken stood there with his hands covered by his jacket, which was draped over where they were cuffed in front of him.

The crowd was fairly dense, and moving around a lot. Because they were standing still, Sam and Ken were conspicuous, and they knew it. Sam had to fight the urge to keep looking around, and keep his eyes on Ken the way he would if he were really the man's captor.

"Ever feel like a bug on a plate? That's sort of how I feel right now," he said softly.

"Yeah, I know what you mean. Sort of feels like the whole world is watching us right now, doesn't it? Of course, they could be, there are enough video cameras around this place to put us on every TV screen in the whole freaking world."

Sam glanced around instinctively, but then caught himself and looked back at Ken. "Video cameras, you say?" he asked. "You mean, like security cameras? The kind that are recorded everywhere?"

Ken nodded. "Yeah, why?"

Sam snatched out his phone and dialed quickly. He whispered a silent prayer, hoping that he had just a few moments to pull off a miracle. He heard ringing through the phone, and then it was answered.

"Sam?" Indie asked. "Sam, are you okay?"

"Babe, I don't have time to talk. Listen to me, and listen close. I'm standing on the National Mall in DC. Right in front of the Lincoln Memorial, in fact. There are security cameras all over this place, is there any chance that you and Herman can hack into them Like, quickly?"

"The Lincoln Memorial? Holy cow, Sam, I don't know. Why?"

"We're about to come face-to-face with Chandler," Sam said. "Now I'll be honest, and there's a chance this could go pretty bad, Baby, but the big risk is that he's got people watching us that we can't see. If you could get into those cameras, maybe you could spot a problem before it becomes one we can't handle."

"I'm feeding Herman even as we speak," Indie said, "and he's pounding all of the video security systems in DC, right now. There's a chance — okay, bingo, we got a hit! Those cameras are monitored by the security office of the National Mall and Parks Service, we're hunting a backdoor now. Come on, Herman, you can do it," she muttered. "Come on, come on — *yes*! We're in! There are, let me see, thirty-two cameras there close to the Lincoln Memorial. All I can do is scan them one at a time, Babe, can you stay with me on the phone?"

"I can for at least a few moments," Sam said. "You're looking for probably two guys together, and there will be something about them that says they're dangerous. If they seem to be talking to their hands, that's a big red flag. Scan fast, and tell me what you see."

"I'm scanning, I'm scanning! Nothing there — nope, nothing there — I'm checking the cameras closest to the memorial first — nothing there — okay, whoa! I've got two men, both of them look like they belong in some spy movie, and I swear they're both trying to hide behind a lamppost. If I've got their position right, then it looks to me like they're looking toward the front of the memorial. Is that where you're at?"

"Yes," Sam said. "Where are they? Which direction from the memorial?"

"Okay, that camera is north east of the memorial itself, so — there's a lamppost just north of the memorial, maybe 50 yards from the structure. Can you see it from where you're at?"

"No, not at the moment, but I'm moving. Ken, move to the north end of the building; Indie sees what may be shooters watching us. They're by the lamppost north of the building. Okay, Babe, I see them. They're far enough away right now that I'm not too worried about them, and I can keep an eye on them from here. Look around and see if you see anything else."

Ken caught Sam's eye. "Sam," he said softly, so that it came through in the earpiece, "we have to take them out."

Sam covered the mouthpiece of his cell phone, and hissed, "No way, there's way too many innocent people around. Besides, if we start shooting, Chandler is going to run. Like you said, he's the important target. Besides, I got an idea." He picked the phone back up to his ear. "Hey, Babe? Can you call the Park Service police here and try to get them on those guys? If you could get the local cops to hassle them for just a few minutes, that would probably cover us."

"That I can," Indie said. "Mom!" Indie called out. "Mom, bring your cell phone. Sam needs your help, call this number and tell them that the two guys in trench coats that are standing by the lamp at the north end of the Lincoln Memorial just tried to rape you."

Sam listened with a grin as Indie's mother, Kim, called the Park Service police and put on an incredible act, hysterically demanding that the two men be arrested immediately. Indie gave him a whispered running account of the act her mother was putting on, and less than a minute later, one of the security golf carts was racing across the grounds towards that lamp. Two officers accosted the two men, and it was obvious that they were going to be occupied for a little while.

"That was great, Babe," Sam said. "Now, do me a favor and keep looking. If you see anyone else that looks suspicious, do whatever it takes to interfere with them the same way. And, Babe? Remember that I love you. I've gotta go." He hung up the phone and stuck it back in his pocket. "Two down," he said softly enough for it to go through the earpiece. "If she sees anymore, she'll do what she can."

"That's good," Ken whispered back. "Chandler is at two o'clock."

Sam looked in the general direction Ken indicated,

and spotted a man wearing a red jacket and a green hat. He checked his position and made sure that he was still pulling off the look he was after, of a man watching another man he was holding prisoner. He kept one eye on Chandler as he approached, but the man stopped twenty yards away and watched them.

"Mr. Prichard," he called out. "I'd like to see your other hand, please."

"That hand's a little occupied," Sam said. He nodded his head toward Ken, who was standing there looking at Chandler as if shocked at seeing him appear there. "As you can see, I kept my end of the bargain. Are you going to keep yours?"

Chandler watched them both for a couple of minutes without saying a word, and Sam didn't push. There was something about the entire experience that was surreal, so strange that Sam wasn't sure if it was even truly happening. He simply waited, just to see what might happen next.

Some activity over towards the Vietnam Wall Memorial caught his eye, as two golf carts of security officers converged on a couple of men who seemed to be lurking behind it. Sam wasn't sure, but he thought it might have been the two they spotted earlier. If they weren't part of Chandler's crew, they wouldn't be hurt by a little delay, and if they were, the delay might help keep Sam and Ken alive. He sent a mental thanks off to Indie, and another one to God for bringing Indie into his life.

He turned his attention back to Chandler who was still watching him. His patience was growing thin, and he was sure Ken was getting pretty restless, as well.

"What's it going to be, Chandler?" he asked. "Do you want to go through with this or not?"

Chandler grinned at him, and then pulled away his windbreaker so that Sam could see the pistol on his belt. "Prichard, neither one of us is stupid. I'm not sure what it is you guys are up to, but one thing I'm sure of is that you're looking for a chance to put me down. Now, I'm not going to give you that chance, and if you go for it, things are going to get very, very ugly. Your friend there wouldn't hesitate to take a shot at me, but somehow I don't think you're quite up to that."

"Play him out," Sam heard whispered in his ear. He moved his own jacket so that Chandler could see the Glock in his hand, then smiled. "I might surprise you," he said, "but I already told you what I wanted. I want to go home, and live my life, without looking over my shoulder for you or your goons. If you can give me that, you can have this guy. Otherwise I'm going to walk away, and that means that all bets are off and you won't see me coming. Maybe you think I'm too much of an amateur to pull it off, but if you've read my file you'll find that I've already surprised a few people. I willing to surprise you, too, but it won't be very pleasant."

Chandler laughed. "Why, Mr. Prichard, you've surprised me already. You're actually standing here, face-to-face with me. Not too many people are willing to do that, knowing the things you know. Now, let me tell you how this is going to go. I've got people watching you right now, and while you may have delayed a few of them — and by the way, I'm really curious how you did that — there are three more you haven't spotted. Two of them have you in the sights of high-powered rifles even now, and the third is merely waiting for me to give him the word. He's another one you'd never see coming. So, as I was saying, let me tell you how this is going to go. Neither of you is going to take a shot at me, because you'd be dead before you managed to aim and squeeze the trigger. I'm not going to take Long with me, because I'm sure you've got something rigged up that he figures will give him the chance to kill me as we leave. I haven't gotten to where I am by being stupid, and I'm not going to start now. So, here's what's going to happen. You're going to wait until I've walked away, and then you and your friend are going to go and find a room. You're going to hole up there until you hear from me. When you do, I'll have something to offer you that you'll both find far too good to turn down. Oh, and just so you'll know I'm telling you the truth..." A bullet, from what was obviously a silenced, high-powered rifle, struck the dirt less than a foot away from Sam's feet. "That's just so you'll know that you don't have a chance of taking me out, right now. Fair enough? Like I said, go get a room and wait. I'll be in touch later today."

Chandler turned and began walking away, and Ken

spun to look at Sam. "Take the shot," he whispered through the earpiece, but Sam shook his head.

"You saw that sniper shot," he whispered back. "We'd both be dead, and that would be the end of the mission. We'll play this his way, for now, and see what we can do to turn the tables when we get the chance. I don't see any other hope."

Ken stood there, staring at Chandler as he walked away, and Sam could tell that he was nearly in a rage, but there was no help for it. If they tried to take him at that moment, all they would accomplish is getting themselves killed. Sam knew that Ken would be angry, but he had to play it the way he felt best.

They stayed put until Chandler was well out of sight, and then Ken flipped his jacket up over his shoulder, showing Sam that he already had the cuffs off. They were in his hand, and he slipped them into his pocket.

"Well," he said. "I don't know what to say. We had him, he was right here. Sam, I know you're no coward, but you should've taken the shot. Yeah, we'd both be dead, but if you'd played it right he'd have gone down with us. I know you want to get home to your family, but Sam, taking him out is worth both our lives."

Sam nodded. "I understand that, Ken, I really do. He didn't walk away because I was afraid, he walked away because I didn't see any hope of getting a clean shot. The second my pistol came into view, my head would've exploded, and you would never have gotten the chance to make a move of your own. They'd have taken you out just to be safe. I had to make the call, so I made the best one I could. If you're pissed, so be it, but it wasn't up to you at that moment, it was up to me. Now, come on; let's get back to the car and go find a room."

Ken shook his head, but he began walking along with Sam. "You know what? You are probably the only man in the world, right at this moment, who could get away with talking to me like that. Whether I like it or not, I still need you. The mission isn't over, and it's going to take both of us to complete it. Yeah, I'm pissed, but I'll get over it. Let's do what we got to do."

It took them half an hour to get back to the parking lot, and Sam was relieved to see that the Corvette was still there. It was, however, drawing a lot of attention, and he spent the next fifteen minutes answering the questions of the four young men who were standing around staring at it. Ken stood over out of sight during this time, his Colt forty-five back in his own belt, so that he could keep a close eye on the situation in case it turned out to be a setup.

Apparently it wasn't. All four of the young men insisted on getting a selfie with Sam and his Corvette. Ken laughed, and shook his head as he got into the car with Sam.

"Next time," he said, "remind me to make sure I pick the car we travel in!"

5

"What a lot of people don't realize is that one hacker can usually see what another hacker is doing," Indie said. "While I was hacking my way into the Lincoln Memorial security systems, I ran across a trail of another hacker who was doing the same thing. Now, this guy is good, but maybe he just wasn't as careful as he should've been, because he left a door open that Herman was able to get into."

Sam had her on speakerphone, and was holding the device out so that both he and Ken could hear what she was saying. "Okay," he said, "so what did you find out?"

"Well, that backdoor led right back into what I'm guessing is your Mr. Chandler's offices. Right now, Herman has a backdoor into the computers there, and it seems like most of them are pounding away on things related to Islamic countries. The user account of the main operator is the one that was doing the hacking, and he spotted Herman poking around inside his computers; now, most guys would have locked it down, tried to kick Herman out. Not this guy, though, he decided to start a conversation. He asked who Herman was, and of course Herman just relayed the message back to me."

"Indie," Sam said, "can this guy track you back to where you're at?"

Indie laughed. "Are you kidding? With this super satellite relay Internet system that Harry's got in his limousine, nobody could pinpoint a location on us. It's not possible. So, knowing that, I sent back and told him that Herman was a friend who wanted him to know that he was working for a very bad man. Here, let me read you off the whole conversation. By the way, his name is Stony. Check this out.

"Stony: well, hello there. Who might you be?

Herman: a friend you haven't met yet. A friend who wants you to know that you work for a very bad man.

Stony: is that so?

Herman: yes. The man you work for is trying to change the whole world so that he has the chance to rule it himself.

Stony: why should you care?

Herman: I don't believe anyone should play God. Do you?

Stony: what does that matter to me? If he rules the world, he'll still need me. Why shouldn't I go along?

Herman: read Revelation chapter 13. Your boss wants to be the Beast. Is that the side you want to be on?

Stony: and I saw a beast rise up out of the sea, having seven heads and ten horns. I've read it. Many times.

Herman: and what are you going to do about it?

"Okay, then at that point he sent me this string of numbers, a time stamp. What that means is that he wants to talk again at a particular time. I ran the time stamp through a converter, and it comes out to a little after five this afternoon. I've kept the back door open, so that I can talk to him again then."

Sam felt a chill run down his spine. "Baby, this is making me nervous," he said. "Why would he want to talk to you again?"

"Well, I'm not sure, but it could be that he knows what his boss is up to and isn't happy about it. I mean, he knew the scriptural reference I threw at him; it's possible this guy is a Christian, or a Bible student, and not a bit in favor of his boss becoming the Antichrist."

"Or maybe," Sam said, "he's just fully aware of what his boss is doing, and likes the idea of being the top computer geek in the world! If Chandler gets into a position to rule the whole freaking planet, then it's highly likely that he's going to take his computer guy with him, especially if the guy has been loyal all along. Are you sure they can't trace you back to where you're hidden?"

"That's one thing I'm certain of, Baby. There's no way in the world anyone could trace me back to here. But,

Sam, my gut instinct says this guy could become an ally. Imagine if we had somebody inside Chandler's offices, how powerful that could be. He's already made it pretty clear that he's not going to make it easy for you guys to stop him. If we could get someone in his organization working on our side, we'd have a better chance of stopping him. Right?"

Ken held out to get Sam's attention. "Sam, she's right. At the moment, you and I are at Chandler's mercy, but as she has a chance to turn someone inside his section and get intelligence that we can use, she's got to go for it. You keep telling me how smart your wife is, well, after this, I believe it. Don't cut her short; she's doing the best thing she can do right at the moment. If she can get anything out of this guy on the computer, we need it, no matter what it is."

Sam shrugged, but then he nodded. "Yeah, I know, and you're right. But, Indie, remember that this isn't like one of our normal skip traces; this isn't the normal hacking you do. These guys are deadly, all of them, and I don't want you taking any chances that could possibly lead them back to you. Do you understand that? Don't take any risks, Babe."

Sam could hear Indie smile through the phone, and knew she was excited about doing her part to help him. "I'll be careful, Honey, I promise. But, Sam, this is too good a chance to pass up. If I can turn Stony to our side, there's no telling what information he could have access to. You stay safe, and I'll call you after I get through talking to him. I love you!"

Sam couldn't help it, he smiled. "I love you, too, Babe. I'll talk to you then."

The phone went dead, and Sam set it down on the bed he was sitting on. He and Ken had checked into a motel on the outskirts of DC, and were waiting to hear from Chandler, as he had instructed them. The clandestine phone that they had used to call him earlier in the day was laid out on the nightstand between the beds, since they expected him to call back on that number.

"That's an incredible woman you got there," Ken said.

"Don't I know it! She's already saved my ass more than once." Sam got up and walked over to the mini fridge, opened it up and took out a bottle of root beer. They had stocked it up with a stop at the convenience store next door to the motel, and Sam looked at the microwavable sandwiches for a moment before choosing one. He glanced over his shoulder at Ken. "You hungry?"

"Yeah, heat me one up too, would you? Sounds like a good idea."

Sam tossed the root beer in his hand over to Ken, then grabbed another for himself while he got a second sandwich out. He popped the packages open, stuck them into the microwave and set the timer for three minutes, according to the instructions on the sandwiches. While they heated, he got each of them a couple of the paper towels they had grabbed at the store. He handed some to Ken, and grinned. "Here, those things get pretty hot in there."

When the microwave *dinged* to tell them it was done, they each got their sandwiches and sat back down on the beds. Ken picked up the remote and turned on the television, switching channels until he found a local news program. They sat through about fifteen minutes of it before they finally caught a report of the five men who were killed earlier that day in the city.

Strangely enough, it was listed as a drug-related shooting incident, and the DC police reported that they had suspects in custody. Sam looked over at Ken, with his eyes wide and his eyebrows high.

"Think that could be Harry's doing?" he asked.

Ken shook his head. "Nope," he said. "That's Chandler. Harry might get them to say it was a drug case, but he'd never convince DC to name a suspect. On the other hand, it's a safe bet that the chief of police probably owes Chandler a favor, or a dozen of them. If he wants those killings to be swept under the rug, some poor schmuck is going down for them. It's that simple."

Sam looked sour. "Doesn't it seem strange to you that somebody could have as much power as Chandler's got, but nobody is doing anything to put a stop to them, except guys like us? To me, it would seem like all of Congress, the president, just about anybody would want to slap this guy down! He's a danger to the whole country, maybe even the world. Why is nobody paying attention?"

Ken looked at him for a moment, and then sat up and leaned forward, resting his elbows on his knees. "Sam, when you were in school, was there a schoolyard bully that took everybody's lunch money, and just did whatever he pleased?"

Sam nodded. "Of course," he said, "Jerry Sheppard. I think every school had a Jerry Sheppard, the guy who shook down all the smaller kids and picked on everyone. And, yes, before you ask, I was one of the guys who stood up to him and got stomped into the ground but that didn't stop me; he never did get my lunch money. Of course, he did stomp me pretty good, now and then."

"Well, Chandler is just a schoolyard bully. The trouble is that he's got the biggest schoolyard in the world, and everyone is afraid of him; he's got so many secrets locked up inside his head, and hidden in God knows how many other places, that everybody who might be big enough to deal with him is scared to death to try. If those secrets get out, then it's a pretty safe bet that all of them will be tarnished, if not destroyed completely. Good grief, even the big political families, the ones who aren't even involved in politics anymore — the Kennedys, the Bushes, all the big names — if he dumps his stash of secrets, things will come out that will destroy all of them, and probably cause most of our history books to have to be rewritten."

Sam grinned. "Maybe that would be a good thing," he said. "Maybe we'd finally find out who was the second shooter on the Grassy Knoll in Dallas, or who really was behind JFK's assassination."

"Nah, Chandler hasn't been around that long, but it's a safe bet that he's got some ideas on who was really behind the attacks on the World Trade Center. You know, an awful lot of demolition experts claim that the only way those buildings could have come down the way they did was with explosives planted on various floors far below where the airplanes hit. There's really not much chance that that wasn't an inside job; you can bet it was orchestrated by people like Chandler. Hell, he may have done it himself. After all, it was supposedly Islamic terrorists, right? And that's right down his alley."

It took Sam a minute to digest all of what Ken had said, and then he shook his head. "Man, you know you're destroying my confidence in the government, right?"

"HA! In that case, I'm doing you the biggest favor anyone's ever done for you. Think about it, Sam, if they have people like me working for them, how far can you really trust them? I'm not a man, I'm a gun; they don't send me out to do a job, they aim me at someone and then they pull my trigger. What kind of government keeps people like me on their payroll?"

Sam stared at Ken for a long moment, and then sighed. "A government that doesn't care about the will of the people. That's what kind."

"Bingo! You just nailed it right on the head." He laid back on the bed again, kicking off his shoes and closing his eyes. "Wake me when Chandler calls, will you?"

"Yeah, right," Sam said. "I think I'm going to take a little nap of my own. Hopefully, one of us will hear the phone."

Sam laid back on the other bed, and threw his arm over his eyes. Within moments, both of them were snoring.

* * * * *

Gary Stone was a nervous young man. Someone had found a back door into the computers that were his responsibility, and he was fairly sure that it would not be good for his employer to find out about it. If there was one thing that he knew Grayson Chandler was fanatical about, it was security. If The Man found out that someone had hacked into his section's computer system, it was a fairly safe bet that Gary would be the one to suffer. Would he survive it? Well, that was a question he didn't know the answer to, and didn't really want to find out about.

The worst part was that the hacker seemed to know an awful lot about what the boss was up to, things that no one was supposed to know, not even Gary. The only reason Gary knew was because, as system administrator, he had access to every part of the network, including private email accounts. Things he had stumbled across by pure accident that led him to install keystroke loggers in the system, along with extremely secure back doors that allowed him to check the logs from outside the office. He could even do so from his phone, and the things he had read that enlightened him to the point that he began to study prophecy all on his own.

Besides having an extremely high IQ, Gary was also an incredibly fast speed reader. Within a week, he knew more about prophecy than Chandler did, and his photographic memory made it possible for him to review the information in a split second. When the hacker had made reference to Revelation 13, Gary had known he was dealing with a serious professional. There were people out there who saw just how crazy Chandler had become, and were trying to stop him. Whoever Herman the hacker was, he had to be working with some of those people. Gary wanted to know more, before deciding whether he wanted to let the boss know about Herman, or join forces with him.

Whatever he decided to do, he would have to make a decision soon. Things were coming to a head, and there were people preparing to do Chandler's bidding, knowing full well that they would be bringing disaster right home to the United States. Some of the things that Chandler was planning now would make 9/11 look like a Sunday picnic. He had almost managed to pull one of them off just weeks ago, when one of the terror cells that his people controlled began planting small suitcase nukes around the country. If it hadn't been for some vacationing private detective, those devices would have gone off as planned, resulting in a nation that would happily give up its freedoms as part of the price of safety and security from future terror attacks. Unfortunately, the plan had been foiled, but then it almost accomplished even more when one lone terrorist went rogue and tried to use one of those bombs to contaminate Lake Mead. It was a brilliant plot, because it would have resulted in millions dying of either thirst or radiation poisoning, it would've caused millions more to relocate out of the southwest US. The overcrowding alone would have cost millions more lives, as people fought over food, water and the simple right to live.

If that single terrorist had accomplished what he had set out to do, Chandler's plans would have advanced by ten years or more. It had come so close that Chandler could taste it, so now he was orchestrating events just as horrific, in order to speed up the process himself.

Ironically, it was that same private eye who had stopped the rogue terrorist, and was now out to stop Chandler himself. It was almost comical, the way this guy kept coming, without even knowing the connection between Chandler and the mission that had almost gotten him killed. As Gary looked through all of the prophecies that were unfolding, he began to realize that there were other things happening that seemed to be directed by an unseen force. The constant reappearance of this private eye was one of them, and while Chandler was determined to get rid of the guy, Gary wasn't sure it was even possible. There was something about this guy,

Prichard, that made Gary wonder if he were exactly the man it would take to bring Chandler's plans crumbling down around him.

All of that led Gary to believe that Prichard might somehow be connected to this Herman character, and if so, Gary wanted to know how that connection came about. If Herman was working for Prichard, or working with him, somehow, then Gary wanted to know it. If it came down to a choice between Chandler and Prichard, Gary wasn't quite sure which side would be the one to be on. All he knew was that there was going to be some sort of a climax coming, and the one thing that was certain was that his world was never going to be the same afterward.

He looked at his computer, and realized that it was time. He opened the connection into the section network, and logged in through the back door that would allow him to communicate with the hacker, Herman.

Stony: Herman, are you here?

Herman: I'm here. What is this all about?

Stony: that's what I want to know. Who are you, and how did you get into our system? What's your connection to all of this, and what do you know about my boss and his plans?

Herman: let's not worry about how I got in. As for your boss, I know that he is trying to set up the new world order that so many people are afraid of. He's trying to make a global government, one that will be run by someone who is nothing but his puppet. Apparently you read the prophecies, so you know just how bad things will get for the rest of the world. Someone has to stop this, and that's where I come in.

Stony: who are you working with?

Herman: who says I'm working with anyone? Maybe I just stumbled across something that I knew would be terrible, and decided to try to do something about it.

Stony: I don't buy that. There are people out to stop the boss now, and one of them has been causing him problems for weeks and doesn't even know it. Does the name Sam Prichard mean anything to you?

Herman: who is Sam Prichard?

Stony: you hesitated. That tells me you know who he is, and that means you are probably working with him. Let's get serious, now. If the boss finds out I'm talking to you like this, it will probably mean my head. But I don't want to see him running the world, and especially not as the Beast. Does your man have a real chance to stop him?

Herman: it would probably mean both of our heads. Yes, I know him. What did you mean about Sam causing problems for your boss for weeks?

Stony: he stopped the suitcase nukes. Boss worked months planning that out, but Prichard managed to stop it, then stopped the crazy one who almost got away with an even bigger bang. Everything I've seen says Prichard doesn't know the boss was behind that, but for some reason he's here in DC and the boss is worried.

Herman: a lot of things are starting to make sense, now. And where do you stand?

Stony: I wish I could say that I stand in a forest in Montana, but I'm a computer geek, not a survivalist. This thing is going to get very bad, and I can either stay close to the boss and ride his coattail, or I can turn against him and hope I choose the right train. If he can be stopped, he should be. I'm just not sure I'm willing to die trying. Get me?

Herman: I get you. Look at it this way, if you side with us you might die trying, that's true. But if you side with him, then there's something worse than dying waiting for you. If you read all of Revelation, then you'll understand what I'm saying.

Stony: yeah, I know. Lake of fire and all that, right? I know what you're saying, even if he isn't the one in the book, he's trying to be. If I were God, I'd lump him right in with the rest, and anyone who helped him. Doesn't really leave me a lot of choice, does it?

Herman: the choice is the one thing you do have. You can decide to help him accomplish what he's trying to do, or you can decide to do what's right.

Stony: and what if he's right? What if he really is the one the prophecy is about, and this is his destiny?

Herman: even if it is, do you want to be on that side? As you said, lake of fire and all that. Is that what you want?

Stony: of course not. I'm not an idiot. This is just a lot to think about. It's scary, you know what I mean? Geez, I'm only nineteen. The boss would cut my throat in a second if he knew I was talking to you like this.

Herman: well, those are the best reasons I've heard yet for you to switch sides. And just for the record, I'm not a whole lot older than you. I just have my reasons for being on the side I'm on.

Stony: it just hit me. One of the reports about Prichard said his wife was a hacker. Don't know how I let that slip my mind, I never forget anything I read. That's you, isn't it? Hello, Mrs. Prichard.

Herman: no fair. I don't know your name.

Stony: tell me something. Does Prichard really have a chance to stop the boss? Or is it going to get me killed if I switch sides now?

Herman: if anyone can, Sam can. If you've read reports about him, you should know that by now.

Stony: yeah, I read them. I know. Doesn't mean I'm not scared, you know? So, if I decide to help you, what do you need me to do?

Herman: I'm just guessing but I think Sam would want any information you could give him that might prove your boss is breaking laws.

Stony: I don't think that would help much. I don't think there's a judge anywhere that would do anything to him. And I know that he has enough dirt on enough people to make sure he wouldn't stay locked up for long.

That isn't the way to do this, if you know what I mean.

Herman: in that case, the real question becomes when and where. When and where can Sam catch him alone?

Stony: check back with me in two hours. I'll give you a decision then.

Herman: okay. Two hours.

Stony: okay. And my name is Gary.

Gary sat back and looked at the screen on his laptop. He wasn't sure how it had come about, but somehow Sam Prichard's wife had hacked into his system. He could go to the boss with that information, and it would probably solidify his position.

Or he could throw in with the Prichards and whomever was working with them to stop Chandler. Considering the enormity of the attacks that Chandler had planned for the next few days, he didn't have any trouble determining what would be the right thing to do; the only problem was whether he had the courage to do it. If he helped Prichard, it meant that he must willingly and knowingly help set his boss up to be murdered. That was a pretty big leap from his normal job as computer system administrator, and since he'd never even thought about doing any kind of "wet work" before, the very idea of it made him a little queasy.

He needed to think, and he only had a couple of hours to come to the biggest decision of his life. He wasn't sure he had what it took to do what Prichard would ask of him, but at the same time, he wasn't sure he could live with himself if he were still with Chandler when he managed to set himself up as a dictator over the entire world. Sooner or later, Gary figured, he was going to come to this crossroad; this decision was undoubtedly part of his own destiny, and he wasn't likely to be able to escape it.

Why did it have to come down to this? No matter how he looked at it, the only way to stop Chandler was by killing him. Could he live with himself if he helped Prichard to do that? Oh, hell, could he live with himself if he didn't?

Gary had worked very hard to be sure that Chandler believed in his loyalty. He'd figured out in his first days on the job that anyone Chandler doubted seemed to disappear, and permanently. He'd put a lot of effort into making sure that Chandler was confident that Gary was a man he could count on, could trust completely. Anything less, Gary knew, would get him killed.

So why in the world was he now sitting here, knowing without any doubt that he was about to make the decision to betray his boss? He had asked Mrs. Prichard for two hours, even though he already knew what his decision would be. Like he'd said, there really wasn't much of a choice, so he was going to do what he had to do.

He went into the secure back door of the system through his laptop, and began reading the keystroke log of Chandler's notes. Everything the man typed, regardless of what program he might be using at the time, was stored in that log, and Gary thought it was kind of ironic that Chandler uses his computer's notepad as a brainstorming device. Every wild idea he had was typed there, and once Gary had gotten used to reading the various kinds of personal shorthand Chandler used, he was able to follow the evolution of each idea from its original conception all the way through to the final plan that Chandler intended to set into motion.

There were three current plans that he was focusing on. The first involved the choreographed assassinations of three European leaders. Those would be the British prime minister and the presidents of France and Germany. Each of these people stood in the way of some part of Chandler's plan to give Islam a greater foothold in Europe. Therefore, they had to go, and he had made arrangements for some small, splinter terrorist groups that were loosely connected to Al Qaeda to use suicide bombers to kill them. Sure, there would be others killed in the blasts, but that was the price you paid when you had to get past a lot of security. In France, for example, there would be four bombers who would all detonate at the same time in different parts of the building where the president would be planning to give a speech. The explosives would be sufficient to bring the building down, killing everyone inside. Mission accomplished.

The second plan involved the sinking of two famous

cruise ships, one from the Princess line, and one of Disney's. In this case, however, credit would be claimed by a small group that was purported to be a remnant of the Branch Davidians, the offshoot Christian sect that was the focus of the Waco debacle in nineteen ninety-three. Immediately afterward, there would be an uproar that would lead to the classification of nondenominational Christianity as terrorist groups. Within days, small, nondenominational churches would begin to be raided by federal agents, who would be looking for any connection to such things as militia groups, the NRA, even any evidence that the members enjoyed hunting. Chandler had already arranged for a federal court ruling that would make it a crime for any nondenominational Christian to own a gun; all the judge was waiting for was word from Chandler that it was time to make the ruling. The result would be a small scale civil war, as militia groups began to stand up at such churches and resist the raids. This would lead to bloodshed, and each incident would lend more credibility to the decisions of the courts.

It was the third plan, however, that had Gary ready to turn against his employer. The first two were bad enough, and the loss of life would be great; the third one made both of them seem like nothing, though.

In just over two weeks, Chandler had the most horrific tragedy that Gary could imagine planned. More people would die than on 9/11, and most of them — because of the emotional impact it would generate —

would be children. Twenty-seven schools were targeted, in different cities around the country. They were large schools, each with thousands of students, ranging in ages from five years up to fourteen. At exactly 9 am Eastern time, all of them would experience the same thing: a gasoline tanker truck, carrying eight thousand gallons of gasoline and a couple of hundred pounds of high explosive, would crash through the doors and into the buildings. The explosives would detonate, rupturing the tanker trailers and sending thousands of gallons of flaming gasoline in every direction. The burning liquid would flow down the hallways and into classrooms, while the flames would shoot up stairways, reaching as high as the third and fourth floors.

Chandler estimated that between forty and sixty thousand children would die, with half of them burning to death and the rest dying of smoke inhalation and heat strokes. The shock would devastate the entire nation, but when the news came out that it was the work of Al Qaeda, the uproar would be greater than any other had ever been, and Americans would begin hunting and killing Muslims in retaliation, leading to a whole new holocaust and threats of war against the United States from every Islamic nation in the world.

And in the midst of it all, Chandler's hand-picked new world leader would arise, ready to bring peace to the world. Within days, the entire world would be amazed at the wisdom and courage of this person, and a clamor would arise for even more counsel. Every nation on earth would work with this new figure, and before anyone realized what was happening, most of them would be recognizing a new order, where Chandler's puppet made the rules, and the world followed them.

It was all in place, and there was only one hope to stop it — and his name was Sam Prichard.

6

Stony: Herman, are you here?

Herman: I'm here. You're right on time.

Stony: look, this isn't easy for me. The trouble is, no matter how I look at it, I can't let things go on the way they are.

Herman: I can imagine. And I really do understand, but things like this have to be dealt with.

Stony: yeah. I know, but it's still not easy. I need to send you some files, do you have a secure protocol we can use?

Herman: give me a minute. Let me see what I can work out.

A couple of minutes passed before Herman came back. Gary was starting to get nervous, but then:

Herman: okay, I hijacked a server that we can use as a relay. Ready for the FTP data?

A moment later, Gary logged into the server Indie had hacked, and uploaded a file that detailed the events Chandler was planning. He told her he'd give her some time to read through it all, and went to his new kitchen to make himself some dinner. Two frozen burritos and a couple of Little Debbie cakes later, he looked back at his computer.

Herman: oh my God.

Stony: yeah. I know what you mean. Now you see why I feel like I don't have a choice.

Herman: this is absolutely unbelievable. I don't know how any human being could do such things.

Stony: it's called power. I haven't been around here long, but I know that people will do anything for power, and this guy has more of it than anyone else.

Herman: okay then, we have to stop him. And we have to do it before he can do any of these things. Did you find me a where and when?

Stony: working on that. I know he's up to something, just not sure what it is. There's some travel planned in the next few days, and I'll see what I can find out tomorrow. Keep this channel open, I don't know when I'll be in touch but I may have to get something to you quickly.

Herman: okay. I'll keep it open. Good luck.

Stony: thanks I'm gonna need it.

Gary read through the chat session again, and wondered how much longer he would live. He was putting his life on the line, and he knew it. If Chandler found out what he was doing, he'd be dead before he even saw it coming.

* * * * *

Indie read through the documents once more, and wiped the tears off her face again. Chandler had already planned the assassinations of three of the most important European leaders, namely the British prime minister and the presidents of France and Germany. He had arranged for some smaller terrorist groups that were somewhat tied to Al Qaeda to take them out with suicide bombers. Collateral damage would be a nuisance, but it was inevitable, so he merely planned to accept it and let it add to the uproar.

Then he planned to sink a couple of cruise ships, both of which would be full of happy tourists from all over the world, and blame it on American Christians. That would give certain politicians the chance to have Christians who weren't affiliated with any of the major sects labeled as terrorists, so that nondenominational churches could be raided by feds. It wouldn't be hard to tie them to things like militia groups and the NRA, so it would be only a matter of time before it would be illegal to belong to one of these splinter churches.

The worst plot, though, was the one that involved burning thousands of school children to death. That was the one she couldn't believe, the one that seemed impossible for any human mind to conceive.

Of course, she realized, it wasn't a human mind she was dealing with. Chandler might be a man, but he was trying to think like a false god, and so he was capable of greater cruelty and atrocity than even Hitler might have come up with.

The things that she was reading just didn't seem real; it didn't seem possible that a human being could conceive such plans, and yet she was looking at proof that one had done just that and she had to get word to Sam, and quickly. She picked up her phone and punched the speed dial for his number.

"Hey, Babe," came Sam's voice as he answered.

"Sam, this thing is so much bigger than we imagined," she said in a rush. "Chandler has got three major events planned over the next couple of weeks, and they're guaranteed to bring us to the precipice of World War Three. He's got it planned out so that just being a member of a nondenominational church will get you listed as a terrorist, and make it illegal for you to own a gun, but that is nothing compared to his big finale. He's planning to hit a bunch of elementary schools with gasoline tanker trucks and bombs, and Sam, he's planning to kill thousands and thousands of kids. He's got it rigged to look like an Al Qaeda or ISIS attack, so that people will start killing Muslims in the streets. All of this is a setup, so that he can have his Antichrist figure step into the spotlight and start calming things down, and he's already got everyone in place to make it happen. Sam this is all going down, we've got to stop it!"

Sam's eyes were wide, and he put the phone on speaker so that Ken could hear it as well. They were still waiting for Chandler to call, and beginning to wonder if he was going to at all. "Indie, go through that again so Ken can hear it."

When she had done so, Ken's eyes were as wide as Sam's. "Holy cow," he said, "I never had any inkling he was that close to making this happen. Sam, you should've taken the shot! It would've been worth it, we should've tried!"

"If we had, we'd both be dead and there would be no one left to stop him. We've got to think our way through this, Ken, not shoot our way through it."

"Well," Indie said, "I've got Gary, that's the computer guy in his office, on our side. He's working on finding out just when and where you might be able to get to Chandler, catch him alone and do what's got to be done. He's the one who got me the files about these plans, and before you ask, I've already sent them off to Harry. I imagine one of us will be hearing from him anytime now."

"Yeah, probably," Sam said. "Chandler's supposed to be calling us, to discuss whatever it is he wants to talk about. We haven't heard from him yet, and we're starting to wonder if we're going to. This waiting is nerve-wracking, but there's nothing else to do at the moment."

No sooner had those words left his lips, then Ken's secret phone began to ring. He glanced at Sam and made a motion like he was cutting his throat, and Sam took his phone off speaker. Ken answered the other one while Sam whispered to Indie that he would have to call her back later. She agreed, and let him go.

"Yeah," Ken said.

"Mr. Long," Chandler said. "Good, I was hoping to get to speak to you. I'm assuming that Mr. Prichard is there, as well?"

"Yeah, we're both here. Tell me what you want, Chandler, and why I shouldn't be trying to kill you right this second."

"Calm down, Long," Chandler said. "You need to get two things through your head: First, that you can't stop me. I'm far too smart for you to outwit, and there isn't anything you can do that will let you beat me at my own game. And the second thing is that this is an opportunity for you. See, I could use a man with your talents, and I'd even be willing to take your friend on, too. He says he wants to be able to live a normal life, but he can live a far better one if he's working with me. There's a new world coming, and if you guys are smart, you can have a place in it. If you're not, then there's no place for you at all. Is that hard to understand?"

Ken made a face. "It's not hard to understand, Chandler, it's just too sick for us to stomach. You're a sick bastard, and a mad dog, and the only way to deal with a mad dog is to put a bullet in its head. I've got yours all ready, and you could make things a lot easier if you'd just let me know where to find you."

Chandler sighed. "You stupid jackass," he said. "I just told you, there's nothing you can do to stop me, so why are you bothering to bluster so much? Good Lord, are you so full of yourself that you actually believe your own press? Ken Long, the Great Assassin—you really ought to find a way to gain some humility."

"I'll be humble the day I see your body laid in a hole in the ground. Until then, you can expect me to stay just as arrogant as you are, you son of a bitch."

"Look," Chandler said, his tone one of condescension. "Let's just agree to disagree, then, shall we? I've already taken steps to be certain you can't get to me, so this is really just a courtesy call, anyway. I'm done playing this game, Long, I've got too many other things that need to be taking up my time. By the time you realize what I'm up to, I'll be so far out of your reach that it won't be possible for you to do anything that could even annoy me, so just go on and find something else to occupy yourselves."

The phone went dead, and Ken looked up at Sam. "He's left the country."

"You can't be sure that," Sam said, but Ken was nodding his head.

"Trust me," Ken said. "The way he was just talking, about being out of our reach? He's gone, out of the country. And I'll guarantee you there's not a trace anywhere of where he went. He wouldn't use commercial transportation; he'd be going on some clandestine or diplomatic flight, and there's no way to find out which one. We blew it, Sam. We just freaking blew it."

Sam stared at him for a moment, then looked down at the phone that was still in his hand. "Maybe not," he said. "Indie's got this guy inside his office talking to her, maybe she can get it out of him."

Ken shrugged. "Maybe she can, if the guy is for real, and if there's anything in the office that will say how Chandler left the country, or where he was going. It's quite possible that he didn't even bother to let anyone in his office know that he was leaving, let alone where he was headed to. That's fairly common in the intelligence community. It's called not letting the left hand know what the right hand is doing."

Sam punched the button to call Indie back, and set it to speaker. When she answered, he let Ken fill her in on what Chandler had had to say.

"Hang on," she said. "Let me see if Gary is still at his computer." They could hear her tapping on her keyboard for a moment, and then she spoke again. "Yes, he's there. Give me a minute to talk with him and see if he knows anything about this."

She fell silent a bit, then, but through the phone they could hear her tapping on her keys. Sam grinned at Ken, who was shaking his head. "Give her a chance," Sam said, "she's a pretty amazing girl."

Ken nodded. "I can tell that, already," he said. "If I had had one like her, you'd be amazed at how different recent history would be. A lot of the things that have happened in the last thirty years might never have happened at all."

* * * * *

Back in Colorado, Indie was having an incredible conversation with Gary Stone.

Herman: your boss has closed and fled the coop. Sam and his partner just talked to him, and they believe he has left the country. Any details on this?

Stony: nada. I hadn't heard anything about it. Are they sure? Let me check some things, give me two minutes.

Herman: okay, waiting.

Stony: well, they're right. He sent an email to one of his people in Libya a couple of hours ago, saying that he would be arriving in Jerusalem tomorrow afternoon. He's apparently hopped onto a diplomatic flight, I don't have any other information than that.

Herman: any idea what he's doing in Jerusalem?

Stony: my guess it's got to do with phase one of the plans I sent you earlier. My gut feeling is that he's going there to start launching the assassinations. I know he's got some people there that he works with from time to time, and I use the term people loosely.

Herman: this is a disaster. There's no hope of getting him back within reach before his plans go into effect, now, is there?

Stony: Mrs. Prichard, let me ask you something. Does your husband want him bad enough to go after him in Jerusalem?

Indie's eyes went wide as she looked at the screen. She picked up the phone. "Sam? He's going to Jerusalem. Gary wants to know if you want him bad enough to go after him there."

Sam and Ken answered in unison. "Yes," they said together, and Ken added, "ask him if he's got any idea on how to get us there."

Indie turned back to the computer.

Herman: they say yes, any idea how they can get there?"

Stony: holy crap I should have known this was going to happen! How do I get myself into these things? Look, the only way I can help them is if I talk to them directly. Give me a number to call them on, then I'll do what I can.

Herman: Gary, can I trust you? This is my husband we're talking about.

Stony: look, lady, I understand how you feel, that we don't have time to play around. Give me a number, or I'll give you mine and you can have them call me, I don't care. Let's just get this thing happening before I chicken out.

Indie sighed and gave him the number, adding a warning that if he did anything that got Sam hurt, she would personally track him down and disembowel him. He sent back a promise that he would do only what he could to help Sam accomplish his mission, and then he was gone.

"Okay, Sam? Look, I had to give him your number. He's going to call you right away and see what he can do to help you. Listen, let me warn you, this guy is just a kid. He's only nineteen, and he's scared to death."

"Okay, Baby, I got it. I love you, and thank you for all your help. I'll be in touch." He hung up the phone.

Sam set the phone down on the nightstand, and got up to grab another root beer from the mini fridge. He had just opened the bottle when the phone rang, and he hurried back to snatch it up. "Hello?"

"So, listen," a voice said nonchalantly, "I was chatting with your wife and she suggested that I might be able to help you out with a problem." The voice was high and squeaky, and Sam could tell the boy was scared.

"Yes, she told me you'd be calling. I want you to know how much I appreciate this. I understand you might be able to help me with some travel arrangements?"

"Yeah, maybe," the nervous voice said. "Do you have passports with you?"

Ken muttered a curse, and Sam groaned. "No, I'm afraid we don't. Is there any way around that?"

"Oh, great," Gary said. "Yeah, we can handle it; I was just hoping not to get that deeply involved." He sighed.

"Okay, look, we're gonna have to meet up. I live in Arlington; how long will it take you to get over here? The address is forty-two ten Eighty-Second Street, apartment 224."

Sam punched it into his GPS, and looked at the ETA. "Looks like we're about twenty-eight minutes from you. Do you want us to come to your place, or meet you somewhere else?"

"Just drive by, and I'll follow you. I know what you're driving, so just keep going and I'll follow. Get out of Arlington and look for a restaurant, we can stop there."

Sam looked at Ken, he nodded. "Okay, and what are you driving? Just so I know if the right car is following me."

"I got a new Mustang, candy apple red. Trust me, I won't be hard to spot. Just get over here, let's get this thing going. I'm scared enough as it is; I don't need to drag it out any longer than necessary."

The phone went dead, and Sam and Ken were up and moving instantly. Not knowing whether they'd be back or not, they grabbed their bags as they headed out the door to the Corvette. They were in the car and on the road less than a minute after the call ended.

The drive to Arlington was uneventful, even though Ken kept looking around, expecting gunshots to come from somewhere. Apparently Chandler had decided that they were no longer a threat, since nobody was coming after them. That was good, but it also showed them just how confident he was that he had beaten them at their own game. Now they were banking everything on a kid who was basically just a computer nerd.

Stopping Chandler was more critical than ever, though, so they would take whatever chances they had to. If it meant they had to trust a nerdy kid in glasses, then so be it. They were on the way to deal with a total nutcase, and needed any help they could get.

"Okay, this is Eighty-Second Street coming up," Ken said. "Turn right, and his place should be about a block up."

Sam turned the corner, and his phone rang. He pulled it out of his pocket and glanced at the display. "It's Harry," he said, and then answered. "Yeah, Harry?"

"Sam, that wife of yours is going to give me gray hair!"

"I don't know how to tell you this, Harry, but it's too late. You've already got gray hair, and lots of it."

"Yeah, whatever. Did she tell you about this file she sent me? Great guns, this guy is such a maniac, I just can't believe it."

"Yeah, she told us. I can't believe there isn't someone we could go to with this information, someone who would have him locked up in a heartbeat. I mean, this is the worst possible kind of treason, but according to Ken there's not anyone who's likely to stand up to him."

"And unfortunately, he's correct. Chandler knows where way too many bodies are buried; no one is going to go up against him as long as he's alive. That's where you boys come in, and Indie has just filled me in on what you're up to now. Jerusalem? For real, Jerusalem?"

"Yeah, that's the way it looks. We're meeting up with Chandler's own computer geek; he says he can arrange some sort of passport and some transportation. Can't say I ever wanted to go to Jerusalem, but it looks like I get to, anyway. Lucky me, huh?"

"Luckier than you think," Harry said. "It's one place I always wanted to go, and never managed to get myself sent to. If I were twenty years younger, I'd trade places with you in a split second."

"What's twenty years got to do with it? I've fought beside you, remember? You probably have a better chance at taking Chandler out then we do."

The car eased past the apartment building, and a bright red Mustang slid out of the parking lot and in behind it. Sam kept going, and the Mustang followed.

"Well, in any event, you let me know if you need anything. If that kid can't get you onto a diplomatic flight, let me know, because I can. I'll also send you the phone number of one of our people in Jerusalem. He can supply you with weapons and other gear you might need once you're there."

Sam was nodding. "Good, Harry, that was one of my concerns. The other is how we're going to find Chandler once we get there. Any ideas on that?"

"I've got a couple people over there I can put to watching him when he arrives. The man at the number

I'm texting to you will know how to reach them, and put you in touch with them. I want you to call me before you leave the country, so we can compare notes. This thing is crazy, Sam, we've got to put a stop to it."

"Harry, we will if it's possible. Just start getting a backup plan ready, just in case. If we go down, somebody has to step up and take over."

"Sam, you're getting me excited. I think I might just decide it's time for me to visit the holy land, myself. If I do, I'll find you, don't worry about finding me." The line went dead, and Sam wondered if the old man were serious or only kidding. Knowing Harry, it wasn't a joke.

Sam kept driving, as the kid had told him to do. It wasn't long before he found himself going out of Arlington, and shortly he was in Alexandria. Ken pointed at a Waffle House™, and he turned in to the parking lot. The Mustang followed him and parked beside the Corvette.

He and Ken got out of the car, just as a short, skinny kid climbed out of the Mustang. The boy wasted no time.

"Okay, real quick," he said, holding up a smart phone. "I need each of you to stand up against the white wall, there, so I can get a picture."

Sam and Ken looked at each other, but the skinny kid with the iPhone didn't look like much of a threat, so they did as he asked. Sam went first, and then Ken took his place as the boy took their photos.

"Okay," the kid said, "let's go in and sit down. We need to be as far away from everybody else as possible, okay?" He led the way inside the restaurant.

They took a booth in the corner, which seemed to be as far from everyone else as they could possibly get. Gary opened up the case he was carrying, and produced not only an ultra-thin computer, but a small printer, as well. He connected his phone to the computer with a cable, and began tapping on the keys and the screen.

"What I'm doing," he said, "is creating a couple of passports. I happen to have some official paper blanks, and I've gone ahead and filled in some basic info, including your height, weight, hair and eye color, things like that that I was able to get from files on each of you. What I'm doing now is adding the photos I just took, so that I can print them out. Don't worry, I've had to do this a couple of times for other people; once it's all stapled together, it's as real as it gets."

Ken looked at the skinny kid. "Who are you, and where did you come from?"

"Gary Stone, and pleased to meet you. No, don't tell me your name, frankly I don't want to know it. It's bad enough, I know his." He pointed at Sam. "Just knowing people like you is enough to get me killed, and I'm trying very hard to live long enough to collect Social Security."

"I don't know why you're bothering, there won't be any money there by the time you're old enough, anyway." Ken grinned at the kid. "Don't you pay any attention to conspiracy theories?"

"Not if I can possibly avoid it," Gary said. "Good grief, man, I live in a conspiracy theory! I'm trying to get away from such things, don't you understand that? And then guys like you show up, and throw prophecies into the mix. There's just no fairness in this, I'm telling you, there's no fairness in it."

Some papers started feeding out of the printer, and Sam leaned over to get a look at them. He saw his own face peeking off the page, but the information beside it said that his name was James Davis. From what he could see, Mr. Davis was from Bakersfield.

"I hope nobody asks me too many questions," he said, "because I've never even been to Bakersfield."

"If anyone is asking that many questions," Ken said to him, "our covers will already be blown and they'll probably be walking us towards the firing squad."

Gary glanced up at Ken, then looked at Sam. "Yeah, what he said. If anyone is getting that curious about you, you're already in trouble."

Sam nodded. "Yeah, I get it. So what can you tell us about this trip to Israel? Any idea who he's going to see there? Any hints on how we can get to him there?"

Gary shrugged his shoulders. "The only address I have is fifteen hundred Chopin Street in Jerusalem. It's some sort of business, but I don't know what. All I know is that we've had to ship things there, so that he could get them when he arrived. I think it may be a safe house, but

I'm not sure. The only thing I can tell you is that it's likely he'll be in and out of there while he's in the city."

Ken leaned forward. "And how do you plan on getting us there? Got that worked out yet?"

Gary grinned. "Actually, I do. You're going as special messengers for the Prophecies Desk. As it happens, I've done a few computer favors for them, and was able to ask for this one in return. Of course, Julie over there thinks that you're my uncles, who have always wanted to go and visit the holy land, ever since you both graduated from seminary. I told her that one of you had cancer, and this was the only way you'd ever be able to make your dream come true, so she agreed. And you guys had better appreciate it, because I'm going to be dating her for the next couple of months, and she's not exactly the prettiest girl I've ever known."

Ken grinned at him. "I'll make you a bet, kid," he said. "If you date her for two months, you'll find she's a lot prettier than you thought she was when you started. Hundred dollars on that, shake on it."

Gary grinned back. "No bet," he said. "I've been through that before, back in high school. Besides, she's one of the nicest girls I've ever met. That's one reason I was willing to ask this of her."

"Okay," Sam said, "So we're your uncles, right?"

"Oh, that's just what I told them over at Prophecies. You don't need to know that for anyone else. All you got to remember is that you, Mr. Prichard, are James Davis from Bakersfield, California, and you, whatever your real name is, you're Stanley Clark from Las Vegas, Nevada. Think you guys can remember those names?"

"Kid," Ken said, "do you know how many names I've used? One more isn't going to matter. I can remember it long enough to get on a plane and off a plane, and that's all that matters to me."

"Good enough. So, anyway, your flight is leaving at 11 pm tonight, from Dulles. Just go to the diplomatic gate, it's not hard to find. Great big sign over it says 'diplomatic gate,' so it shouldn't be a problem. Your names – the names on your passports, that is — will be on the list at the gate, and they'll have your boarding passes for you. Incidentally, if you've never been on a diplomatic flight, then here's a word of advice. Don't drink the champagne."

"Why not?" Sam asked, and Ken began to laugh.

"Because, they don't serve champagne on diplomatic flights. It's an initiation that they like to try to pull on newbies, and just trust me when I say you don't even want to know what's in that glass. If it's offered to you, just smile and say no thanks."

Sam looked from Ken to Gary, and shook his head. "Okay," he said. "Somehow, I think I'd better just take your word for it."

Gary nodded. "You'll be a lot happier if you do."

Suddenly, Ken burst out laughing, and pointed at Gary. "I get it," he said. "You fell for it, didn't you?"

Gary looked at him, and glared. "Do you want these passports, or not?" He finished assembling them, then produced a stapler and hit each one twice. He folded them and handed each to the man whose picture it contained. He turned back to his computer and began tapping keys again.

Sam looked at him. "What now?"

"Those passports won't do you much good, without ID to back them up. I'm generating you each a new driver's license, under the name on your passport."

Sam shook his head, and looked hard at the computer and printer. "Good grief, kid, is there anything you can't do with this rig?"

"Yeah," Gary said. "I can't print money with it. Well, actually, I could, but sure as I tried, I'd get caught. Somehow I don't think I'd do well in federal prison, and besides, I get paid pretty good to do what I do."

"Well, I'm glad you do," Sam said, "and at this moment, I'm just glad you're on our side."

Gary looked up at him. "Let's get something straight," he said. "I'm not on your side, I'm on my side. It just so happens that the interests of your side and my side coincide at this moment. And I'm not sure I could say that again to save my life."

7

Ron Thomas tapped on the door to Harry's office, and waited to be invited in, as always. It was almost nine o'clock in the evening, but Harry was sitting at his desk when he entered.

"Ron, my boy," Harry said, "tell me something good that I really want to know."

"Harry, you know I would if I could," Ron said in return, "but I just don't have anything that great. I checked out that kid you told me about from Chandler's office, and you're right. He's one I'd love to have on our team. Think there's any chance we can get him?"

"Well, if things go according to plan, he's going to be looking for a new job real soon. I'll make a point of putting in a request for him if that opportunity becomes available. What about those travel arrangements I asked you for? Did you get those worked out?"

"Well, yes and no. The quickest I could get you into

Jerusalem will be the day after tomorrow. There's another diplomatic flight going out tomorrow afternoon, and I can arrange to get you there in time to get on it. You'll hop a military shuttle tomorrow morning at 6 am, and that will get you to Dulles for the dip flight. It leaves around two in the afternoon, so you would arrive in Jerusalem day after tomorrow, about 10:30 am, their time."

"Good, make it happen. The most important mission in the history of the world is going down over there, and I'll be darned if I'm going to sit here and miss out on it. Even if I get there late, at least I can say I was there for the mop up. That's better than nothing, I guess. Any word from Sam?"

Ron scowled. "Harry, you know good and well that he doesn't bother calling through the switchboard. He calls you on your cell phone, and is probably the only person I know of who can get away with that as often as he does. Sometimes I wonder if he's your long-lost son or something."

"He's not, but I'd claim him in a heartbeat if he was willing. There's something special about that boy, and I'd be lying if I said I didn't love him like he was my own. But don't get your feelings hurt, Ron, Boy, I feel the same way about you, you know."

"Oh, goody," Ron said, "I can claim two of the deadliest men in the world are my emotional family. Gee, Pop, can I borrow the car this weekend? Huh?

Can I, can I? Huh?"

"Don't act like an idiot, Ron, you know how I hate that. Anything else?"

"Nope, I just wanted to fill you in on the flight. You know, you probably ought to get some sleep. You're going to be in the air early in the morning, and you won't get much chance to rest before you arrive in Jerusalem. You're talking nearly twenty hours in the air, altogether."

Harry looked up at Ron and smiled, reaching out to stroke his Colonel Sanders beard. "Well, and I can probably do that if you would get the heck out of my office. Go on, Son, I'll be fine. Who's taking me to the airport?"

"That'll be me," Ron said. "George and your car are still out at the cabin in the mountains."

"And that's exactly where I want them to be."

Ron knew a dismissal when he heard one, so he turned and left the office. As soon as he was out the door, Harry picked up his cell phone and punched the button to call Sam. Sam answered on the first ring.

"Hey, Harry," he said.

"Tell me something good, Sam," Harry said, almost echoing the words he had said to Ron just moments before.

"Well, we just checked in for a flight to Israel, and no one is looking at us funny, so I guess we're ahead of the game. I got your text message with the number for your man in Jerusalem. Anything special I should know about that guy?"

"Only that I've given instructions to follow your orders as if they were my own. Anyone who knows me, knows I wouldn't say that unless I have the utmost confidence in you. My people there will have weapons and just about anything else you might need, and they should have an idea of where Chandler is by the time you arrive."

"All right," Sam said. "I don't know anything else to tell you, not at the moment. Ken is sitting in a chair, sound asleep. I wish I could do that, but I'm too stressed out. Listen, Harry," Sam hesitated, then went on. "Harry, if anything happens to me..."

"They'll both be well taken care of, Sam. I made those arrangements the minute you left for DC. In the past, I've always had a strong gut feeling that you would survive whatever got thrown at you, but I'll be honest and tell you that this time, I'm scared. Scared enough that I'm getting on a flight for Jerusalem myself tomorrow afternoon. I'll be a day behind you, but I'm coming."

Sam grinned. "You old fart. You just don't want to miss out on the excitement. Just don't expect us to wait for you; if we get a chance to take Chandler out. After seeing what he had planned, I think it's a tossup which one of us wants to put the bullet in his head the worst."

"No, it's not. I'm quite certain, Sam, that you want to kill him worse than either I or Ken, simply because you have a baby girl at home that you know and love.

Neither of us ever had that luxury, so while we might be infuriated that Chandler would target children, we can't feel it the way you can. Just remember that it doesn't matter who gets the shot; it's just important that someone does. Chandler must be stopped, no matter what the cost."

Sam nodded into the phone. "Don't worry, Harry, I know that. And I won't let you down."

"Why, Sam — you never have." The line went dead.

The woman who had checked them in for the flight suddenly picked up a microphone and announced that they were boarding. Sam reached over with a foot and kicked Ken's chair, waking him up. "Come on, Stanley. They're singing our song."

Ken got up, rubbed a hand over his face, then picked up his bag and followed Sam down the ramp and into the airplane. Most of the aircraft was allotted to cargo space, for diplomatic shipments; there were only a couple of dozen rows of seats, so they grabbed two side-by-side. Sam was a little quicker, and got the window seat. Ken didn't seem to mind, because he buckled his seat belt and was snoring again within seconds.

Sam took out his phone and called Indie one more time, telling her and Kenzie how much he loved them and promising their daughter that he would be back home as soon as possible.

"And, Daddy," little Kenzie said, "be sure you don't get shot again. I don't like it when you get shot."

"Don't worry, Sweetheart," he said. "I'll do my best. I love you."

"I love you, too, Daddy," Kenzie said. Sam said goodbye to both of them, and turned the phone off before the plane began to move away from the terminal. A part of him was terrified that he might never see them again, but a bigger part was terrified of what would happen to them if he failed in his mission. He closed his eyes and uttered a prayer that God would help him to achieve what he had to do.

Suddenly the plane began to move down the runway, and then the nose came up and the rumbling stopped as the wheels left the earth. Sam felt the bumps as the landing gear was tucked away, and he was on his way to Jerusalem.

* * * * *

The flight made one stop, in Germany, where it stayed on the ground for less than twenty minutes. Two passengers and several parcels got off the plane, and then the doors were shut while the plane was refueled, and then it turned around and was back in the air again. A flight crewman — there were no flight attendants on board — offered Sam and Ken brown paper bags that each contained a couple of turkey salad sandwiches, a bag of chips and a banana. On the other hand, there was a cooler full of soft drinks, and they were told to help themselves to all they wanted. Sam dug through the ice for a couple of minutes before he concluded that there was no root beer, and settled for a Coke.

There weren't a lot of people on the flight, and most of those who were seemed to be sleeping a lot. A couple of people tried to strike up conversations, but Sam and Ken made it clear they weren't interested in being friendly. Sam felt a little rude, but it was safer than making a mistake that would give away the fact that they were phonies.

They both dozed in and out as the plane flew on through the air, and finally woke up the last time when the pilot announced they were making their descent towards Ben-Gurion airport at Tel Aviv, Israel. Sam sat up and watched out the window as the plane came down, and finally touched the runway.

This time, the plane taxied all the way to the terminal. It parked near what Sam guessed was the equivalent of the diplomatic gate, and some portable stairs mounted on a truck were driven up to it. A flight crewman opened the door, and everyone was allowed to disembark.

An Israeli policeman was waiting at the bottom of the stairs to guide them all to the appropriate line for diplomatic visitors. Because they had diplomatic passports, none of their bags were searched and they did not pass through customs, but were led to a table where a bored man glanced at their passports, stamped them and waved them on past. Five minutes after climbing down the stairs, Sam and Ken were climbing into a taxicab.

"We're going to Jerusalem," Ken said, "the King David Hotel. See if you can get us there without racking up a ridiculous charge, and I'll throw in a hefty tip. How about forty shekels?"

The driver smiled and nodded vigorously. "King David Hotel," he said. "King David Hotel, yes, yes!" No sooner had they shut the doors then the car lurched forward, tires squealing as the driver hurried to collect his tip.

Sam looked over at Ken. "The King David Hotel?"

"Yeah, it's a pretty nice place. I figured, what the heck, I've got a couple of cards that still have some money on them, we might as well stay somewhere nice. After all, we're here to save the world, right?"

Sam chuckled. "I guess so," he said. "Think I should call Harry's friend now? Or wait till we get settled into a room?"

"I'd wait, I think. I think that would be best. It's not that late in the day, so we can take the time to get a bite to eat. I don't know about you, but those sandwiches just didn't do it for me."

Sam nodded. "Yeah, I have to say I could sure use something decent. Can you get a good steak in Israel?"

"The best," Ken said. "Trust me, there's a restaurant at the King David that will put a steak in front of you that will make you drool, and when you taste it, you'll think you've died and gone to Heaven."

"Okay, fine, but shut up about it until we get there. I'm starving!"

The ride took about forty minutes, with the driver being careful not to take any detours, or rack up any extra miles. Sam took out his phone and called Indie to let her know they had arrived safely, but it was only 6 am in Colorado, so he told her he loved her and let her go back to sleep. A moment later, his phone rang and he saw that it was Harry.

"Good morning, Harry," Sam said.

"Son, I'm about to get on the plane that will take me to Washington. Sometime after I get there, I'll be getting on another plane that will be chasing the one you just got off of. When I get the chance, I'll call and find out how things are going for you there, but just expect to see me sometime tomorrow, before noon."

"Assuming we're still alive," Sam said. "I'm looking forward to it, Harry. It's about time you got off your lazy rump and got back out here in the field with us grunts. Do you want us to try to pick you up at the airport?"

"No, I'll make my own way to wherever you are. If you've already got the mission accomplished, then will simply celebrate together. If not, then we'll see what I can do to help."

"Sounds good. See you then." As always, the phone went dead before Sam could even say goodbye.

When they pulled up in front of the hotel, Ken simply tossed the man a fifty-dollar bill and got out.

From the look on the driver's face, Sam concluded that he was happy to see it.

"They take American money here?" he asked.

Ken nodded and smiled. "They love it," he said. "The exchange rate is about four shekels to the dollar, for an Israeli national. If you or I tried to exchange dollars we'd only get about three and a quarter shekels each. When he exchanges that, he'll end up with almost two hundred shekels, as opposed to maybe a hundred shekels if I'd paid him that way."

"No wonder he was smiling," Sam said. "Sounds like a pretty good racket."

They entered the hotel, and Sam was impressed at its splendor. He was even more impressed when he realized that Ken was paying over four hundred dollars a night for their room. Knowing that the card Ken was using was a phony, and had come from one of his prior assignments, he didn't say a word, but just kept a smile on his face as if he belonged there.

Even though they only had carry-on luggage, a bellman was assigned to show them to their room. They rode up the elevator with the bellman talking nonstop, offering to get them tour guides, special accommodations, which was another way of saying, "I can get you anything you want." They thanked him, but refused any special services, and Ken slipped him a twenty-dollar bill as soon as he opened the door of their room for them.

"Can't say I wasn't glad to see him leave," Sam said. He looked around the room, and whistled. "What a place," he said. "I thought I'd stayed in some nice hotels, but none of them compare to this."

"Yeah, I've been here a couple of times. It's always a nice place to stay." He walked through the room, checking all of the amenities. It was actually more of a suite, with a sitting room and a separate bedroom. There was a king-size bed in the bedroom, but the sofa in the sitting room folded out to one that was just as big, and almost as luxurious. "You can have the bedroom, Sam. I'll stay out here."

"Okay, but there are some things we need to do first. First off, I'm gonna call Harry's man, and arrange for some weapons and Intel. Then, you're gonna show me where to find that steak. After that, if nothing else is going on, we can worry about who sleeps where."

He took out his phone and dialed the number that Harry had given him. It was answered a moment later, and Sam was surprised when he heard a woman's voice on the other end of the line. "Hello, a mutual friend gave me this number and told me to call when I got here."

"Oh, then you must be Samuel. Yes, I've been expecting your call. I have a package for you, and if you tell me where you're staying, I'd be happy to bring it to you."

"Oh, well — okay, then. We're at the King David Hotel, room 640. I think we're going to get a bite to eat, would you be joining us very soon?"

The woman laughed. "Why, yes, I can be there in about fifteen minutes. Is that an invitation to join you for dinner? It's a little early for me, but I wouldn't mind."

"Yes, it is. We'd be happy to have you join us, and perhaps you can fill us in on some of the events happening here in the city that we need to be aware of."

"Oh, I'm quite sure I can. And as I said, I have a package for you, anyway. Very well, I'll be there in fifteen minutes. Perhaps we can meet in the lobby? Near the concierge? I'll be easy to spot, because I'll be wearing a dress. This time of year, most ladies will be wearing slacks. Oh, and I'm a blonde."

"Okay, then, we'll see you when you get here. Oh, can I get your name?"

"Sure. It's Natasha. Be there shortly."

Sam hung up the phone and turned to Ken. "Well, Harry's man is a woman," he said. "I invited her to join us for dinner; hope your phony credit card can handle that. She said she's bringing a package for us, and will bring us up-to-date on what's going on. We're supposed to meet her down by the concierge in about fifteen minutes."

Ken nodded. "Okay. That doesn't leave us time for a shower, but we probably ought to change shirts, at least."

Each of them did so, and Sam took the opportunity to run a razor over his face. All of that took up ten minutes, so they left the room and took the elevator down to the lobby. The concierge desk was surrounded by chairs and couches, so they went over and took seats. They'd only been there a couple of minutes when a lady entered, a blonde-haired lady in a modest dress, carrying what looked like a salesman's sample case. She glanced at the two of them and broke into a grin, while Ken suddenly groaned.

"Natasha Minsky," he said. "I'm gonna kill Harry when I see him."

The woman walked directly to them, so Sam and Ken stood. She smiled broadly, looking at Ken. "Why, Kenneth," she said. "Harry didn't tell me you were coming. If I'd known, I could've baked a cake."

Sam looked her over. She was a blonde, all right, but it was the kind that came out of a bottle to cover gray hair. She was also, if he was any judge, at least in her mid-fifties. Ken looked up at him with a weak smile. "Natasha and I have worked together in the past, on an assignment in South America. Remind me to tell you her history, someday."

Natasha waved a hand as if to dismiss the past. "History is not important," she said. "What most definitely is important, however, is your current mission. Harry sent me a lot of information, and I've been doing some digging on my own, as well. This monster has to be stopped, and right away. His first moves are scheduled for within the next forty-eight hours, but that's as close as I can pinpoint them."

Sam looked down at the case she was carrying.

"Should we take that up to the room, or take it into the restaurant with us? I don't know about either of you, but I'm ready to eat."

"We can take it along. I've got some files in it that you might want to look at while we have dinner. And yes, I'm starving. I don't usually get to eat this early, but I missed lunch today so it's kind of a blessing for me."

Ken pointed across the lobby to the entrance of the restaurant. "The La Regence," he said. "Sam wants a steak, and their fillet of beef financier is going to be the best steak he's ever met in his life. Shall we?"

They entered the restaurant, and at Ken's request, they were seated in the corner, off by themselves. The waiter took their orders and then left them alone, and Ken asked Natasha to give them an update on Chandler.

"We've got three people keeping him under surveillance," she said, "and they're very good at what they do. They switch out often, and change clothing and hair so that he never realizes it's the same people. He's made two stops, one in Tel Aviv, and then one here on Chopin Street. That's where he's been for the last few hours, and from what we can tell, it must be his local headquarters. If he leaves, I'll be notified, and I'll pass the word on to you."

She had opened the case, and withdrew two files which she handed over, one to each of them. "The first photo you see there is the building on Chopin. It seems to be some sort of office building, but no one seems to know much about it. Some small company that does public relations work, that's all we can get."

"What about security, bodyguards? Is he moving about alone?" Ken asked.

"No, he has an entourage of five or six people with him. They were waiting when he got off the plane, and our people said they were with him the entire time until he got to Chopin Street. We have to assume they'll be with him if he leaves, as well. There are photographs in the folder, showing him and the entire group."

Ken flipped through the photos, as Sam did likewise. Sam, of course, didn't recognize any of the faces except for Chandler's, but Ken let out a curse.

"What's wrong?" Sam asked, and Ken muttered the same word again.

"See this guy?" He pointed at a tall man in the photo with Chandler. "That's David Glenn, the one I was telling you about. When Chandler told Harry that he had gone rogue, I assumed that Chandler had him put down. Obviously, I was wrong, and I can tell you that he is one formidable opponent. Chandler uses him for assassinations, but his real specialty is personal security. He's very good at keeping someone safe and alive, and I'm sure that's why he's with Chandler right now."

"Well, let's face it, that would make sense. He may not know we've come to Jerusalem after him, but he knows that there are people out to stop him. He's gonna want whatever security he can get."

Ken was nodding. "Yeah, it's just going to make it a little harder to get to Chandler. And it would be a safe bet that the rest of those men are David's hand-picked people. None of them will be easy to get past."

Sam leaned forward and looked Ken in the eye. "I'm going to tell you something. I'm not a bit worried about getting past those people, because if they get in the way, I want to go right through them. As far as I'm concerned, if they're working with him, they are just as bad as he is. If I have to take a page out of his book, and blow them all up to get to him, that's fine with me."

Natasha grinned and looked at Ken. "Your friend, here, has the same fire in him that you used to have. Remember Venezuela? That's how you felt about Torres, and you got him. I was impressed."

"Sam has a lot on the line on this mission," he said. "He has a wife and little girl back home, and he wants to get back to them. At the same time, he knows what will happen to them if Chandler manages to pull off what he is up to. That's what gives him the fire, but I'm hoping to help make sure he gets to see his family again."

The woman turned and looked Sam over. "There must be something special about you," she said. "Harry Winslow told me I'm to obey your orders just as if they were his. He's never given me instructions like that before, so that tells me he has the ultimate confidence in you. Now, frankly, I'll do as he says, but I don't know you like he does and so I don't have that confidence in you. If you get me killed, Sam Prichard, I'm going to be so pissed off at you!"

Ken winked at Sam. "Word to the wise, don't get her killed. She's a former Soviet agent, came over to our side after the fall of communism. If there's one thing she knows how to do, it's hold a grudge. I don't think even death would be enough to keep her from getting her revenge."

"I'll bear that in mind," Sam said. "So, Natasha, do you have any ideas on how we can get to Chandler?"

She shook her head. "Not at this moment, no. Right now, I'm waiting for my surveillance team to let me know when he moves again. That may give us some opportunities, and that's all I can hope for, don't you agree?"

Sam shrugged. "I just want to put a stop to this madman, and at this point I don't care how I do it. He's a mad dog, and the only way to deal with a mad dog is with a bullet in its brain."

"What about hardware?" Ken asked. Natasha picked up the case, and tilted it so that Ken could see inside, and then did the same for Sam. He saw that there was an assortment of weapons in the bottom of the case, and nodded his approval.

The waiter brought their meals, and they switched to small talk as they ate. Sam made so many moans of Epicurean delight that Ken began to chuckle at him. "That's pretty good, isn't it?" he asked, but all Sam could do was nod his head vigorously as he continued to chew.

The meal was delicious, for all of them, but soon it was over. Natasha accompanied them up to their room, and they spent some time looking at other parts of the file she had brought. There were photographs that showed the building on Chopin Street from different angles, including from the roofs of nearby buildings. "I've thought of putting snipers up there, to try to take him as he leaves, but from what I can tell, it looks like there may be cameras watching those roofs. Up on top of that building, in the photos, can you see those things that protrude upward? I believe that those are security cameras, so I think any activity on the nearby buildings would be detected."

Both of the men nodded, agreeing with her assessment. "I think," Ken said, "our best bet is going to be trying to catch him on the street. If we can get him while he's in a car, or moving from vehicle to building, then we have a chance of making a good strike. I don't want to miss, because I don't think we'd get a second chance. This guy knows so many secrets that he's surely been the target of assassination attempts in the past, so the very fact that no one has taken him down says he's a pro at anticipating and surviving them."

"Agreed," said Natasha. "But you also can't forget that he is playing on prophecy. Jerusalem is the center of the three greatest religions on the earth, so given the chance, there's no doubt in my mind that he would attempt to make his actions appear to fulfill some prophecy. Now, according to Harry, Chandler is into some old Babylonian/Mesopotamian prophecies regarding the sun god, Shamash. Those prophecies also predict the rise of a Beast-like figure, but without the appearance of Jesus at the end of his reign. His followers believe that he will rule the world for the rest of eternity, and will in some way become immortal because of his allegiance to the sun god. If Chandler gets the opportunity, I'm sure he'll try to take anything we do and fit it into one of those prophecies."

"I'm not concerned about any fulfillment of false prophecies," Sam said. "As a Christian myself, I follow the view of the biblical prophecies, including those in the Book of Revelation. If it should turn out that Chandler truly is the false prophet, the second Beast of Revelation, then so be it. From what I've learned, if that's the case then the Rapture should be coming any day, and my family and I won't need to worry much about it. The problem is that I don't believe that's the case, so this madman is trying to force things to happen outside of their time. In order to do that, he's willing to sacrifice literally thousands of lives, including the lives of many thousands of children. That would make him the greatest murderer in history, in my book. Granted, there have been genocides that have killed more people, but I can't imagine any single murder event that could kill so many, and have such a devastating impact upon an entire nation as his plan to wipe out all those schools."

Natasha nodded sadly. "I agree with you," she said.

"But while you would hate to see so many of your children die in that attack, I don't believe you have seen the big picture. By laying the blame for it upon radical Muslims, Chandler will be launching a whole new form of warfare upon the Islamic people. Every American, especially the many thousands who will be connected personally to the children who die, will be ready to see Muslims die in retribution. Thousands of your people will take up weapons and begin to murder every Muslim they can find, in the belief that they are somehow avenging those who have been lost. This is Chandler's true plan, for it will cause Muslim nations to demand action against your country, and it could lead to a third world war. It certainly will, if something doesn't happen, but that is the rest of his plan. His puppet, whoever it is, will suddenly arise with the answer that will bring peace. Every nation that is screaming for your destruction, because of Chandler's control over those in power within them, will accept that puppet's suggestions and agree to some form of peace. Other nations' leaders, also under threat of some kind of exposure by Chandler, will similarly bow to this puppet. With so much support, it will be a matter of no more than weeks or months before the world is ready to accept that person as some type of global leader. Any nation that resists, will of course face extinction, for it will not be able to stand against an army of millions, an army made up of the armies of a dozen nations, or more."

Sam shook his head. "And thus is ushered in the

New World order. You know, I understand that the true Antichrist will be a monster as far as his actions against the people, but at this point I have trouble imagining anyone who could be a greater monster than Grayson Chandler."

"Well, now you know why I've been trying to stop him for a couple of years," Ken said. "I didn't have any idea just how bad he could get, just how evil he truly is, but I knew that he had to be stopped. I was just concerned about the threat to our national sovereignty, but this — this evil is so far beyond anything I had imagined that I — all I know is, he has to die."

8

Sam left Ken and Natasha talking in the sitting room, while he went to take a shower. The long flight had left him feeling less than fresh, and he wanted to get into some clean clothes. When he got out, he got to take a look at the weapons Natasha had brought them.

There were an identical pair of silenced nine millimeter pistols, as well as a pair of heavier forty caliber Glocks. Sam was delighted at these, especially when he found three additional magazines for each pistol, and two boxes of extra ammunition for each.

In addition, in the bottom of the case, he found a box that he opened. Inside was a weapon he'd never dreamed of, a strangely modified Colt forty-five government model that, when assembled, would have a longer barrel in the shoulder stock. A laser sight tucked under the barrel would presumably give this weapon some incredible accuracy at medium range. This was a

140

carbine, a short-to-medium-range sniper's weapon, small enough when disassembled to smuggle into a building under normal clothing, but powerful enough to do the job. A pair of long, thirty round magazines were provided, and both of them were full of forty-five caliber ACP rounds.

Since Ken was still busy talking, Sam chose the pistols he wanted and left the others. He showed Ken the carbine conversion, and saw the smile that it brought to his face.

"I haven't used one of those in a long time," Ken said. "They can be pretty sweet, especially when you need to get into a tight spot to shoot from."

"I can imagine," Sam said. "I think it would be pretty sweet, as you say, if we got a chance to use this on Chandler."

Ken shrugged. "We might. On the other hand, I'd give my left arm for a good fifty cal sniper rifle, right now. I could just about reach out and touch him from here with that."

"Sorry, boys," Natasha said, "didn't have any of those in our arms room. When I looked at what was available, I felt like what I brought was the best selection."

"Relax, beautiful," Ken said. "No one is complaining, just wishful thinking. This is one of the most important targets I've ever gone after, and probably one of the most difficult. I'd happily take a SCUD missile, if I knew I could reach him with it."

"Sorry, I didn't have any of those, either. To be honest, it didn't occur to me you might want explosives. I do have grenades, and I believe there are some LAWS rockets. Those can do some damage to armored cars and tanks, so they might be useful against a normal sedan. If you want them, I'll get them for you."

Sam looked at Ken, but he only shrugged. "It's almost impossible to guess what you might need," he said. "Carrying rockets and grenades around is much more dangerous, and considerably more noticeable, than just packing iron in the form of automatic pistols. Even that carbine is easier to conceal down your britches than grenades or rockets."

A phone rang suddenly, and Natasha pulled one from her purse. "Hello? Yes, this is she. All right, keep me posted. Let me know if he stops for any length of time, and where." She ended the call, and Sam was reminded of Harry. Like him, she didn't even bother to say goodbye.

"That was the surveillance team," she said. "Chandler and his people are on the move. They climbed into a van and seemed to be headed into the business district. They're keeping them in sight, and will let me know if he stops, or changes direction."

Sam got up and began pacing around the room. "Okay, that's great that there watching him, but that doesn't really help us. We should be out there, on his tail ourselves. That way, we can take the shot when the opportunity comes."

Ken shook his head. "It isn't that easy, Sam. It's not like you see in the movies, where the secret agent is always on top of the bad guy. In real life, we spend a lot of time just watching and waiting. If we can get some idea of a routine, or if he stops somewhere we can be certain he'll stay for a while, then we can make a move. Until then, we wait and let the Intel come in."

"I hate waiting," Sam said, and then he went and stood by the window, looking out over the gardens and pool.

The afternoon wore on, and although there were more reports from the surveillance team, none of them were helpful. The only thing that seemed to be of value was when one of the team managed to get close to Chandler and overheard him telling one of his people that they would be meeting up with someone important late the following afternoon, and a particular restaurant was named for the meeting.

"There it is," Ken said. "That's our opportunity, our window. We can be there, waiting for him, since we know he'll be there tomorrow. Natasha, where's this place at?"

"It's actually not far," she said. "It's off of King George Street, in the downtown triangle. I know the place; it's not very big, and the front is open to the street."

Ken furrowed his brow. "That's odd," he said. "It sounds like the perfect place for an ambush, so I can't imagine why he would choose it. That's almost like saying, 'Here I am, come and get me.' I can't imagine why he would choose such a place, it doesn't make sense."

"Maybe it does," Natasha said. "Depending on who it is he's a meeting there, it could be that the choice of meeting place was theirs and they chose this one so that they could see a threat that might be coming. I mean, nobody really trusts Chandler, they're just afraid of him. Right?"

Ken shrugged. "That's true, and it's possible that someone else chose the location. It's even possible that it was chosen specifically because it would be a good place for an ambush. Maybe someone else is planning one."

"Somehow, I don't see us getting that lucky," Sam said. "I think that's just more of your wishful thinking."

Natasha stood and faced them both. "Well, either way, it doesn't matter," she said. "It's still the best opportunity we're going to get, so we need to go and look it over, figure out how to position for the morning. Maybe we can even find ways to use the other weapons."

Sam shook his head. "No, no rockets, not into a restaurant. I understand there may be collateral damage in missions like this, but I want to avoid any we can, all right? Same for grenades; they'll be fine if we can use them against him, or even his little group, like in a car or something, but not in a public setting."

Natasha turned to Ken. "Great, you brought Opie

Taylor with you. Harry swears by this guy, Ken, but I'll be honest—if he can't handle it, you should have left him behind."

"Shut up, Natasha," Ken said suddenly. "I've already fought beside Sam, and I trust him, too. If you've got a problem, then go on home, and we'll handle this alone. Otherwise, just help us do our job. And without any further commentary, all right?"

Sam was watching them both, and suddenly started laughing.

"What's so funny?" Ken asked, and Sam laughed even harder for a moment.

"I was just surprised," he said, "because you said she used to be a Soviet agent, but she knew who Opie Taylor was! I had to stop and think for a minute, before I remembered that Opie Taylor was the kid from the old Andy Griffith show! That's old Americana, Man, it just cracked me up that a Russian spy would use it like an old American would."

Ken and Natasha both looked at him as if he had lost his mind, so he just shrugged and turned back to looking out the window.

An hour later, they'd come to the conclusion that the restaurant offered the best possible opportunity to get a shot at Chandler, so they agreed to go for it. They followed Natasha down to her car, and she drove them to where the restaurant sat on King George. Since they knew that Chandler and company were all safely tucked away back on Chopin Street, they parked the car and went inside.

The place was about thirty feet across, and twice that in depth, with the entire front wall made of glass doors that slid into the walls on either side. When it was cold, they could be closed, but since the weather was warm, they were open. Several of the tables had been dragged outside, onto the sidewalk, and there was a festive atmosphere inside the place.

They took a table near the back, and ordered soft drinks, with Sam delighted to find that the place carried a brand of root beer, called Virgil's. It was stronger than what he was used to, but it was root beer, and he was happy.

"I'm thinking," Ken said, "that if we could get a spot over there, across the street, we could probably get a pretty clear shot at him no matter where he might sit in here. The only problem is how to position ourselves so that he won't see us. Any ideas?"

Natasha stared at the area he was indicating. "What about a truck, like a delivery truck? UPS, something like that?"

Ken shook his head. "Too obvious. Anything that he can't see into is likely to make him turn and run. I know it would, if it was me. No, we need something that won't look like it could be hiding us, but still does."

Sam was also looking at the spot, and an idea was trying to form in his mind. He let it settle, and then grinned.

"Hey," he said. "You're not thinking it through all the way. You're thinking of how to hide us while we take the shot, right? Well, why hide at all?"

Ken looked at him. "Well, not getting shot dead before we get our jobs done comes to mind as a pretty good reason. What are you thinking?"

Sam pointed. "The whole front is open onto King George Street. If we wait until we know he's inside here, we could come in and start blasting right at the front door, basically. We'd have the element of surprise, and if we could get hold of some automatic weapons..."

Natasha nodded. "I can get H-K machine pistols, ten millimeter. They're pretty nasty, especially up close like this would be. The problem I see is that if you drive up here in a hurry, by the time you get out of the car, his bodyguards are going to know who you are and they'll be able to open fire before you can."

"True," Sam said, "if you drove up in a car. The sound of the engine, the doors slamming open, all of it would give you away. On the other hand, if we were just hiding up the street a little ways, we could wait 'til they were inside and sitting down, then just stroll up at our leisure and walk in with our guns blazing. It's the same way the Chicago mob used to get rid of their opposition; they didn't bother with anything fancy, they just walked in and started firing point blank. If it worked for them, it ought to work for us, too."

Ken looked around, and then nodded. "It's worth a try," he said, "but I don't like the idea of putting all our eggs into a single basket. I'll make the hit, with you waiting as backup. With a pair of those machine pistols, I should be able to take the whole lot of them out in about eight seconds."

Sam was shaking his head. "I don't like that idea," he said. "I think we should go in together, and get it done. We can't take a chance on him getting away, Ken, we just can't."

"Sam, it's a suicide mission. It won't matter if I get them all, at least some of them are gonna get me, too, and I don't see any way around that. I don't have a family waiting at home, you do. I go alone."

Natasha reached over and laid a hand on his. "Kenneth, are you sure? As you say, it's suicide. Oh, you might survive, but only if we can get you to surgery in time. Think it through, before you commit."

"I'm already committed, Natasha. This guy has to be put down, and this is the best shot. If I fail, then Sam will still be out here, and can try again. It's the best way."

Sam stared at him for a long moment, then nodded once. "Okay," he said, "you're the pro at this thing. I'll be the backup—but, Ken, I don't want you to get yourself killed, especially if you can't get Chandler. Don't throw your life away unless it buys us what we need, which is him in the grave. Deal?"

"Deal," Ken said. "Let's get out of here. I feel like a

drink, and this isn't where I want to have it."

They got up and left, then went back to the hotel. Ken planned for them to be in position the next afternoon by four, so that they'd be ready when Chandler showed up, but that left him a lot of hours. They went to the hotel bar, and Ken ordered a whiskey sour.

After five of them, he finally allowed Sam to drag them back up to the room. He didn't even bother to fold out the couch, but just flopped onto it and passed out.

Sam went into the bedroom and called Indie. She was delighted to hear from him, and he was careful to keep his voice and manner light.

"Hey, Babe," he said. "Just wanted to hear your voice before I hit the hay. What's Kenzie doing?"

"She's gone with your mom; they went to get some groceries. George and one of the men went with them. She'll be upset that she missed your call."

"Well, you tell her that I love her, and that my work here might be over tomorrow. If it is, then I hope to come home the day after that. How's everything else there?"

"It's going okay," she said wistfully, "but I wish you were here. Sam, this is the craziest thing that we've ever been mixed up in, and it scares me. I'm terrified something bad is going to happen."

"It'll all be okay, Babe," Sam said. "Ken says I'm just the second string, here, and he gets to go take care of the job. Like I said, if everything goes according to plan, we'll be done here tomorrow afternoon, and then I'll be on the way home to you." He sighed. "I think I'm ready to go into music full time, what would you think of that?"

He heard something that sounded like a cross between a laugh and a sob, but the smile in her voice was unmistakable. "Sam, that would be my idea of Heaven, right at this moment!"

They chatted for a few minutes longer, and then said their 'I love you's' to one another. Sam hung up, and whispered a prayer that it wouldn't be the last time he ever heard her voice, then climbed into the bed and laid there for an hour before he got to sleep.

Sam woke the next morning, looked at his phone and saw that it was nearly ten in the morning, and wondered how much sleep he still needed in order to feel human. He didn't worry over it for too long, though, because he knew where he was and why he was there, so he rolled out of the bed and went to the sitting room to check on Ken.

He had risen earlier, and left a note saying that he'd been down in the restaurant, having breakfast. Sam washed his face and went down the elevator to find him. When he saw him sitting in the same spot where they'd had their dinner the night before, he waved and joined him.

"I figured you'd be here on time," Ken said, "so I ordered you some coffee. Be warned, it's strong and nasty, compared to the stuff we're used to."

"As long as it has caffeine, I'm happy," Sam said, but he grimaced after tasting the coffee. He picked up a sugar bowl and added several spoons to the cup. "What's good for breakfast here?"

"Get the *shakshouka,*" Ken said. "It's poached eggs in tomato and veggie sauce, and it's awesome! And tell them to add a side of herring."

Sam looked at him doubtfully, but ordered the meal when the waiter came. When he'd gone, Ken looked at him and smiled.

"I wanted to tell you," he said, "that I've really been glad to get to know you, Sam Prichard. You're an amazing fellow, and a good man to have at your back. If things go bad this afternoon, I want you to know that."

Sam scowled. "I still wish you'd let me go in with you. Together, we might have a chance to get it done and survive."

Ken smiled. "I'd rather know you're ready to back me up and make sure Chandler dies, if for any reason he escapes me. That's the most important thing you can do for me, Sam, I'm serious. I need..."

Sam's phone rang, and he pulled it out of his pocket. "It's Harry," he said, then answered.

"Hey, Harry."

"Sam, I have now realized a lifelong dream, and landed in Israel. I'm in a taxi and on my way to Jerusalem, so where the heck are you?"

"We're at the King David Hotel, Harry, and sitting in the restaurant. How far out are you?"

"I'm guessing that I can be there in about thirty more minutes," Harry said. "Stay there, and you can buy me something to eat; I'm famished."

The line went dead, and Sam put the phone away. "Harry's here, and on the way. I can't wait to hear what he thinks of this plan."

Ken smiled. "He'll hate it, but so do you, so that's no surprise. I'm more worried that he'll try to put the kibosh on it. I'm going in there after Chandler, Sam, and neither of you is gonna stop me, got that?"

"Hey, I'm not arguing," Sam said. "I just think you're an idiot, but there's nothing new about that. Maybe Harry can talk some sense into you."

Harry came walking into the restaurant a half hour later, and Sam waved to show him where they were sitting. He waved back and made his way through the tightly packed tables to get to theirs, and sat down. He looked at Sam's empty dishes and blinked.

"Tell me they have steaks here," he said, and Sam laughed.

"Get the fillet of beef, Harry, I had it last night and it's incredible."

Harry placed the order when the waiter appeared, and then Sam and Ken began filling him in on the plan to hit Chandler that afternoon. Harry asked a few questions, nodded at the right places, and finally said,

"Sounds to me like the best way to go about it. When you call Natasha, tell her we need a third machine pistol, though."

Ken scowled. "Harry, I'm going in alone, I already explained that to you."

Harry looked at him. "Did I say anything different? I simply want to be armed, in case the bastard gets past you and comes running my way. Do you blame me?"

They took Harry's bag up to their room when he'd finished eating, and he took the chance to lie down for a short nap on the couch. They were scheduled to meet with Natasha there at the room at two, so Sam and Ken went and shared the bed for a couple of hours, themselves. When they rose at one thirty, they found Harry up and using a laptop computer to study the area around the restaurant.

"I've got it all figured out," he said. "I see how you want to handle this, Ken, and I think it could work, but look at this: Here, right to the north of the restaurant, there's this little narrow alley. It's just about wide enough for us to hide in single file, and it's invisible from the street. I'm thinking that if Sam and I were in there, then when you go in from the south end, we could strike from the opposite side. They wouldn't know for at least a few seconds what hit them, so we'd have a good chance of making the hit and coming out of it with all of us alive."

Ken stared at him. "You're not gonna let me do this my way, are you, you old bastard?"

Harry grinned at him. "I've been in this business a lot longer than you, Son, remember that? Besides, there are times when you just have to do something, and I'm having one of those times. I need to be in on this, Ken. Just deal with an old man's stubbornness, okay?"

Sam laughed. "You can't beat him, Ken, you might as well just face it. We're all going to be in on this, and it's gonna be better that way."

The three of them talked over the plan until they were all sure of what was expected of each of them, and by the time Natasha showed up, they were ready to get rolling. She gave Harry a hug, and kissed his cheek, then handed him the machine pistol he'd demanded.

They piled into her car, and she drove them to the restaurant so that they could all get into position. They knew that it would be a long wait, but they felt better about being there early, and each of them had spent long hours in waiting before. It wasn't anything new to them, and they were all able to find a way to get comfortable.

Ken sat on a rock behind a bush that was about twenty yards from the place, while Harry and Sam had to sit down on the ground. Each of them had an earpiece in that Natasha had provided, so that when the surveillance team saw Chandler coming their way, they would be notified a few minutes early. That way, they could all get to their feet and be ready to move once all their prey was inside.

That call came at four forty, and the three of them

readied themselves. One of the watchers confirmed that Chandler was in the car when it pulled up in front of the restaurant, and that he did get out and enter the place. Harry held up a hand to keep Sam from moving too quickly, and then he motioned for them to go.

They came around the north side of the entrance just as Ken came around from the south, and all three of them saw the group of men that was sitting at the table in the back. Chandler looked up at them, and his face registered shock at the site of Ken and Sam, and then Sam raised his gun and began firing. Chandler and his own men began shooting back, and Sam saw Chandler drop to the floor, and then Harry came around him, and everything was happening fast.

There were several other people in the place, and they all began screaming and trying to run, and Sam was shoved aside by a man who was holding a child. He caught his balance, and leveled his gun once more, but then another man ran into him and he fell to one side. He hit a table, and slid off of it to the floor, and for a split second he was looking Chandler in the eye, but before he could even react, there was a foot coming down on his face. He pushed it off, and a man fell beside him, but Sam was fighting his way back to his feet. He tried to move forward, to get to Chandler, but a burst of gunfire came at him out of nowhere, and he ducked instinctively.

Something hit him again, and he fell onto another table, but by the time he could get up and see what was going on, the place where Chandler had been was empty. Four of his men were down, including David Glenn, but Chandler was gone. Sam spun around, looking for Ken, and saw him on the floor, his shirt covered in blood. He started toward him, but stepped on something, and when he looked down, he saw that he was stepping on Harry.

There was a bloody spot on Harry's face, and as Sam looked at him, he saw that blood was oozing out of it. Harry's mouth was working, but there was an odd look in his eyes, and Sam suddenly forgot about Chandler, forgot about Ken. He dropped to his knees and pulled the old man up to himself, and listened to see what Harry was saying, but it was too faint.

He looked down at the old man, and as he did, a blankness came over his eyes, and Sam stared at him.

He looked up and saw Ken, who was trying to get to a sitting position, and then he heard the sirens. He looked back down at Harry's lifeless face, and suddenly wondered if maybe Chandler really was the Beast.

And then he began to cry.

BOOK 8
DRIFTER: PART THREE

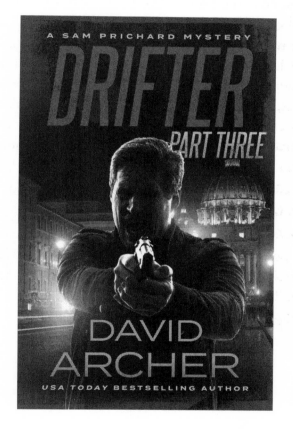

AVAILABLE ON AMAZON

ABOUT

David Archer was born and raised in Bakersfield, California. He is a fiction author and novelist, writing in the mysteries and thrillers genre. His approach to writing is to hit deep, keep you entertained, and leave you wanting MORE with every turn of the page. He writes mysteries, thrillers, and suspense novels, all of which are primed to get your heart pumping.

The author's books are a mixture of mystery, action, suspense, and humor. If you're looking for a good place to start, take a look at his bestselling Sam Prichard Novels, available now. You can grab copies in eBook, Audio, or Paperback on all major retailers.

Made in the USA
Coppell, TX
09 May 2020

24323150R00097